JOHN WAYNE COMUNALE

Cover Art by CV Hunt

Thanks to Nick P for pointing out the sinkholes of life and how to plug 'em.

-JWC

4

1

The sinkhole started after all the rain from the hurricane, but we didn't know it was a sinkhole at first. It rained so much, and for so long, it took the backyard over a week to dry out, and even then the grass was so thick and high you couldn't tell if one spot was lower than the other. Especially since it started out so small.

It was Betsy who noticed it first, but only because she went to the back of the yard to coax a little black cat she called Sandman into her arms with a small pinch of catnip. The cat escaped often by squeezing himself through windows left cracked open, or by running through your legs just as you opened the door. Sandman always came back, but that never stopped Betsy from going to look whenever she discovered him absent. Betsy loved that cat more than me and everybody else, and she had no problem letting you know that was how she felt.

She came through the back door and into the kitchen, cradling that cat like it was a newborn baby of her own flesh and blood. I was sitting at the table drinking coffee, while flipping through the newspaper trying to find any article that wasn't in some way related to the storm, but tales of its rampant destruction still filled nearly every page of every section.

I finally landed on a story about an upcoming Poodle Fair taking place over the weekend at the VFW hall. I didn't know what a Poodle Fair was, nor did I believe I would have any interest in one, but over the past two weeks I'd read more about the storm than I'd read about all other forms of weather throughout my entire life combined. Today was as good as any day to learn about a Poodle Fair. I'd barely gotten through the first sentence when Betsy walked in, squawking at me before the screen door had a chance to slam behind her.

5

"There's something weird in the backyard," she said, louder than she needed to, as she passed through the kitchen, still stroking Sandman.

"What?" I said, looking up from the paper for clarification, but she was already in the next room out of earshot.

I was set to ignore her and carry on with my coffee and poodles, but as I brought the mug to my lips, Betsy stuck her head back in.

"I said there's something weird in the backyard!"

Her voice was louder now because Betsy hated to repeat herself in general, but even more so, she hated repeating herself to me. A lifetime of loud music and working in a machine shop had affected my hearing some, but as far as Betsy was concerned I might as well have been stone-deaf. Most of the time, I just pretended to hear her, just to avoid setting her off.

Besides, most of the time, not hearing had nothing to do with it; the speed at which she said things was what made her difficult to understand. This time in particular I heard her just fine, and my response was for reasons of clarity and context. I waited a beat before asking a follow up question, hoping she'd elaborate without prompting. She did not.

"Well ..." I had to holler now because Betsy had ducked back into the other room. "... what exactly is this weird thing?"

Betsy's muffled voice barely projected past the door, so I put down the cup of coffee I'd yet to take a sip from, pushed away from the table, and went to the other room where she was fussing with the eight-foot tall, carpeted-covered monstrosity of a cat-house that lived in the corner. The cat was tightly nuzzled against Betsy's chest in a repurposed sling meant to hold newborn babies. She looked over to acknowledge my entrance, then turned back to what she was doing.

"Well?" she said.

"Well what?"

"Well, what are you going to do about it?"

"About what?"

"Reggie Aaron-Lee Mayer." She used my full name as if she were scolding a child. "I swear you need hearing aids. I asked what you were gonna do about the weird hole in the yard."

"So it's a hole?"

"No, not a *hole*, hole." She paused, furrowed her brow, and scrunched her nose and mouth together, indicating she was thinking. "It's not a hole exactly, but it looks like it wants to be one soon."

I loved Betsy with all my heart, but when she said things like this it made me question her critical thinking skills.

"What the hell is that supposed to mean?"

Betsy stopped and turned to face me, holding the cat tightly to her chest with one arm while emphatically gesturing with the other.

"It means it wants to be a hole, but it ain't all the way there yet, Reggie," she said matching my own annoyed tone. "Okay? That's what it means."

She turned back to the cat-house structure without waiting for me to reply or ask any additional follow up questions to further clear up her vague description of what she deemed to be 'almost' a hole. I debated continuing the pointless back-and-forth for a little while longer, mostly so I could get the last word in, but decided against it.

The scathing quip poised to spring from the tip of my tongue wouldn't be worth the amount of grief I would have to endure in return, so I swallowed my remark to save for a day I felt like arguing. I hadn't even had a sip of my coffee yet, and already I was debating the semantics of what may or may not be a hole.

"All right," I said, upset with myself for how defeated-sounding my tone was. "I'll head back there and check it out."

"Thank you Reggie," sang Betsy, without turning around.

She hummed as she whisked a brush back and forth across a section of the carpeted cat mansion. She kept that cat's house up better than she did our own, and I was pretty sure the

7

goddamn thing was eating better than me. More than once I've smelled something delicious coming from the kitchen, only later to find my dinner was a cold turkey sandwich with generic, deli-style chips on the side.

I trudged back to the kitchen, hoping Betsy didn't catch a whiff of the derision I felt over the duty she'd tasked me with, and I stopped to finally take a sip of my coffee. It was already stone cold.

I dumped the coffee out into the sink and went to reach for the pot for a refill, then thought better of it, deciding to wait until after I'd taken a look at this so-called soon to be hole. Otherwise, I wouldn't be able to fully enjoy it or my Poodle Fair. I pushed through the back door, stepped out into the yard, and scanned for abnormalities. Nothing looked out of the ordinary to me from where I stood, but then again I didn't know what 'almost a hole' looked like.

Rather than yell back in for Betsy to tell me exactly where she saw this indecisive patch of earth, I just walked the yard to find it myself. The thought of enduring another exchange with Betsy over the matter made my head hurt. All it would do was waste the morning, and put more space between my coffee, the poodles, and me.

I went down the center of the backyard, keeping my head on a swivel to look for uneven patches in the ground. I realized I was walking at double my usual pace mostly out of frustration, but also trying to be efficient. A thought occurred to me about a quarter of the way into the yard. I was frustrated over having my time interrupted with the impromptu chore, but I hadn't stopped to think Betsy might have actually seen something worth being concerned over. For some reason, and out of nowhere, I remembered an article I'd read five maybe six years ago. It had been about something called sinkholes, and how several of them had opened in Florida, swallowing cars and houses whole.

There was a woman in the article who reported seeing a sinkhole open up beneath her neighbor's home, plunging it hundreds of feet down into some eternal, hellacious darkness. What if what Betsy saw wasn't an aspiring hole, but the start of a sinkhole like the ones I'd read about? I looked down at the ground, taking my time to search for any abnormalities, but the grass was so thick it was hard to notice any difference.

Our house hadn't taken any damage during this storm, but it had in one ten years back, and dealing with the insurance company had been a pain in the ass. Only a portion of the roof and about of a third of the gutters on the back side of the house were damaged, and it was for the most part cosmetic. Those bastards nickel and dimed us to death between our deductible and depreciation, and weeks went by before they finally sent a check.

I didn't even want to think about the hassle they would give me if I called in a claim for the house falling into a sinkhole. If that's what I was indeed dealing with, I was going to have to research how to reverse it, or fill it, or whatever you do to fix it before it develops into a Hellmouth.

I stepped forward gingerly, trying to will my body to be lighter than it was, just in case I was unknowingly skirting the edge. I started to scan the ground in front of me again, slowly, then looked right and realized I needed to look no further.

Ten yards to the right of where I stood was an obvious indentation in the ground. The high grass around it worked to camouflage the depression unless you were standing in just the right spot, which was why I hadn't seen any difference in the yard at first. I moved toward it to get a better look, no longer worried about being sucked into the ground since I had the area in my sights. Still, I couldn't fight back the odd sense of dread that suddenly pulled my stomach down to my shoes.

I stood at the edge of the indention and stared down to survey it further. I was never the best at judging space and distance, but off the top of my head I thought it looked to be at least three or four feet in diameter. It was in the shape of a mostly perfect circle with a few sharp edges jutting out in an attempt to claim more ground. This gave me cause for worry, since I figured it was a sign the hole was spreading. While I had

10

never seen a sinkhole in person, I was now convinced I was looking at the start of one.

The drop-off around the edges was only about an inch or so down from the rest of the yard's level, but closer to the center it dropped down to what I thought looked like five or six inches. The height of the grass made it hard to tell exactly, but the glimpse I could get between blades told me it was at least that deep if not deeper.

I touched the tip of my toe along the edge like I was testing the temperature of bath water, being careful not to put too much weight down. The ground felt softer than the rest of the yard, but I could still feel what I would consider solid ground beneath. I mustered the courage to tap my toe a few inches further on, and felt the soft ground give under my foot. I jumped back as the same sense of dread screamed at me to not only get away from the hole, but to get away from the entire area.

For a moment I contemplated running around the front to my truck, jumping in, and driving as far away from my own home as I could before something horrifying happened. Betsy and her cat would have to fend for themselves, and quite frankly she'd probably prefer it that way.

I pushed the thought away, realizing complete abandonment was not a viable solution to this problem. I got an idea and began to look around for any sticks or small branches that might be lying around. The longer, the better. A few seconds later, my eyes landed on what I was looking for, and I headed to the far left corner of the yard where some broken branches were leaning up against the fence. I selected the thinnest of the bunch and stood it up next to me so I could better judge its length.

According to my driver's license, I was five foot ten, although a year or so ago Betsy told me I was not that tall and insisted on measuring me. The conversation of course resulted in the usual argumentative back and forth we'd adopted as our primary form of communication. The fierce exchange climaxed with a measurement that revealed I was in reality only five foot nine. The argument ended with Betsy telling me I needed to go

11

to the DMV to have it changed because lying on a government document was a federal offense. I thought she was full of shit, but I ended up changing it anyway on the off chance she was right and would have the opportunity to say *told you so* at a later date.

The busted branch came up to my chin, and I deemed it long enough to serve the purpose I had in mind. I stripped the leaves and small sprouting offshoots as I walked back to the sinkhole to test a theory I hoped I was wrong about. I stood a few inches back from the edge, not feeling any safer about it, and brought the branch down next to where I had felt my toe sink into the ground.

I pushed down and the branch slid slowly and easily into the earth. When I felt resistance, I yanked it up, and turned it upside down so I could get a better look at how far in it had gone. What I thought was only four inches looked to be closer to six, or maybe even seven, but I had nothing available to compare it to for reference. I turned the branch back toward the sinkhole, moving the dirt-caked end closer to the center before gently pushing down.

The branch sank into the ground without me having to apply pressure, and the dread reminded me it hadn't gone anywhere. I pulled it out quickly, unsure of how to proceed, and the tip came out with a slurpy pop. I scooted back from the sunken edge a few more inches, hoping to give myself some peace of mind that did not come.

I took a deep breath, bent my knees for no other reason than I'd heard people say to bend your knees when doing physical things to avoid injury, and moved the branch back over the center of the sunken area. I forwent the slow descent approach and shoved the branch down with some force behind it. I realized this was a bad idea when the branch easily breached the ground, plunging deeper and deeper with no resistance to counterbalance what I pushed with. I stumbled forward toward the edge as not inches, but feet of the branch disappeared beneath the surface.

I realized I could let the branch go and released the death grip I'd had on it. I was able to halt my forward momentum by digging my heels in just as my toes crested the sunken edge, but I still couldn't catch my balance. I managed to direct my fall off to the side of the sinkhole; my face landing inches from the edge.

I watched all five-plus feet of the branch disappear into the ground with the ease of an all-pro linebacker running through a pop-warner offensive line. Too frightened to get to my feet, I rolled away from the hole back toward the house. When I deemed I was far enough away, I staggered to my feet, tripped and fell back down, but managed to get upright on the second try. I sprinted to the back door, and didn't realize I was screaming until I was in the kitchen.

3

Betsy raced in from the other room, and the look of terror on her face snapped me from my panic. She clutched the cat, still in a sling made for human babies, tight to her chest with one hand and covered its ears with the other. I stopped to lean on the counter, grabbing my chest as I tried to catch my breath.

"What in the absolute hell are you hollerin' about, Reggie!?" Betsy's tone was that of anger and not concern. "You're upsetting Sandman!"

I glared at Betsy while sucking wind, trying to get enough control over my breathing so I could answer. She didn't bother hiding her impatience, motioning with her hand for me to 'hurry it up' and still not bothering to concern herself with my wellbeing. If I had a heart attack in front of Betsy, she'd be so disinterested she'd leave and say she'd come back after I'd finished up.

At least I'd be dead then, and free of the non-stop bickering our lives together had become. I'd never have to see that damned cat living higher on the hog than the man of the house. Death would be a sweet release, of that I had no doubts, but while it may come for me soon, it wasn't my time presently. I would have to continue carrying this cross for at least another day.

"Damn-," I gasped, finally able to choke out the word. "Dammit Betsy, can't you see I'm trying to not die? Let me . . . let me catch my breath!"

"Well, you're the one running in here hollerin' like the sky is falling!" Her face was still void of concern, and her lips had curled into a snarl, indicating her anger level had risen several notches.

14

My breathing finally slowed enough for me to gain the control I needed to fully regulate my speech. Even though I knew I could speak, I waited an additional twenty seconds before I did in spite of Betsy's demeanor.

"Sinkhole," I said. "That's what it is, a goddamn sinkhole."

I glanced over at the newspaper still lying open on the table, but I was afraid Poodle Fairs would forever remain a mystery to me. I had much more important things to occupy my mind, like how to keep from being swallowed by my backyard.

"Sinkhole? What's a sinkhole?"

Her ignorance and matter-of-fact way of asking the question acted as a one-two punch of aggravation through my ever-thinning patience. I didn't know if Betsy was truly oblivious to what a sinkhole was and the danger that went along with it, or she did know and was downplaying the seriousness of the situation for no other reason than to be contradictory of me. Knowing Betsy, I would guess the latter.

"What's a sinkhole?!" My tone was patronizing and sarcastic, but would prove to backfire on me. "A sinkhole is a . . . Well, it's like a hole but . . . it's not . . ."

My aggravation doubled when I realized I couldn't properly articulate exactly what a sinkhole was, and Betsy glared with judgment.

"So, are you saying it's not a hole, but it wants to be one soon?" Her tone dripped with venom and cynicism.

I flashed back to the way she'd attempted to describe the sinkhole to me not thirty minutes earlier, and cursed my inability to communicate the ins and outs (no pun intended) of a sinkhole effectively. I attempted to push the panic from my mind for just a second, with the hope I could locate a succinct definition lodged away in the depths of my brain, but I couldn't get past the image of our house dropping into the depths of the Earth.

"Reggie!" Betsy snapped, derailing my dueling trains of thought.

15

If circumstances were different, and I wasn't playing beat the clock against my own possible death and the destruction of everything we owned, I would have turned this into a fight. I hated to relent to Betsy on any issue no matter how large or small, but self-preservation took priority over winning an argument at the moment.

"Fine," I shouted, throwing my hands in the air. "That's exactly what it is, okay! You were right! What's out in the yard is *not* a hole, but most certainly will be one soon, and it's going to be one mother fucker of a hole at that!"

Having to stare down her smug expression was like taking a javelin in each eye, but it was the right decision. She still held the cat close against her body with one arm, but was now using the other to slowly and gently caress the thing's back while shaking her head and clicking her tongue. This was her trademark body language signifying I was about to be on the receiving end of a lengthy ear-beating.

"Reggie," she said, her tone low and even. "You know I certainly do not appreciate that language, and furthermore --"

"I know, I know," I interrupted, "and like I said you're right, but I don't have time for this right now. When that thing decides it's ready to become a full-fledged hole we're gonna find ourselves in a shit-heap of trouble if we don't act fast."

Despite Betsy not liking my use of foul language, the flash of anger faded from her eyes. I guessed she was able to pick up on the serious panic in my voice.

"I don't see what the problem is." Betsy was still stroking the cat, and speaking in a tempered, matter-of-fact tone. "Just go down to the lumber yard, and get a few yards of dirt to fill it in. There's no reason to be yellin' and screamin' bloody murder over a thing like that."

"I'm afraid it's not going to be that easy to take care of," I replied, now matching her softened delivery. "I don't think the lumber yard has enough dirt to sell me."

"Well, just keep driving around until you find one that does." She was aggravated again, her words becoming sharp and

16

pointy. "*Or* call around before you leave so you don't have to make unnecessary stops."

Never had I needed to suppress my urge to instigate an all out shouting match expounding upon the flaw in her logic, but I stayed myself once again. There was simply no time to try and win an argument right now.

"Betsy," I started, "a sinkhole isn't just a hole you fill up with some dirt from the lumber yard. Now, while I don't know exactly how they start, I do know what the end result looks like. All I can say is somehow or another the area beneath our backyard has been . . . hollowed out. At least I think it has, or something like that."

"How did it get hol-"

"I told you, I don't know, and if I did I still don't have time to explain it to you. Basically, at any moment the entire backyard could become one giant hole, and drag us, the house, and even your precious little cat down into it."

Betsy hugged Sandman closer to her chest with both hands now, and I could tell she didn't appreciate me bringing him into this.

"Okay Mr. Answer-man," she said. "What do we do to fix it then?"

I honestly hadn't thought that far ahead. Trying to explain the sinkhole was hard enough, while fixing it was something else altogether, but fighting was not going to help the situation or either one of us. For the second time in less than an hour I did something I hated to do. I was going to take another stinger to my pride and *not* argue with Betsy.

As much as it pained me, I'd rather be alive to argue later than be plunged into death and darkness trying to make a point. I took a deep breath, leaned back against the counter, and pinched the bridge of my nose to stave off the oncoming headache that came every time I surrendered to Betsy. I honestly thought that by this point in our lives I would have died from an embolism exploding in my brain because of it, but no such luck. At least not yet.

17

"Look," I said lowering my voice, "I'm sorry for yelling. I'm not . . . I'm not exactly sure how to fix it. All I know is that these things are dangerous. We need to do something, and we need to do it fast."

A wrinkle of concern folded across Betsy's forehead, signaling I'd finally gotten through to her. She stroked the cat again, but this time the action served to soothe her.

"Okay," Betsy began slowly. "I didn't realize how . . . dangerous it could be, but I believe you."

The tenderness in her voice was something I hadn't heard since the early years of our relationship together. Nineteen years of marriage and daily bickering had eroded that tenderness into an icepick of bitterness she used to stab my ears bloody every day. Not that I hadn't played my part in driving the wedge of distance and disagreement between us over the years. All of it melted away now as we stood in agreement on something for the first time in longer than either of us could remember.

"Maybe we should call the city? Or maybe even the sheriff?" Betsy took a step toward me with genuine concern growing in her widening eyes.

I wanted to take her in my arms, hold her tight, and tell her everything would be okay, but the hopeless dread began to bubble up again from beneath my guts. I turned away to face the sink, and looked out the window into the backyard. What had been hidden by high grass before was now quite visible from where I stood.

The sinkhole had grown.

4

"Yeah, I'm gonna have to call this into the city."

The pot-bellied sheriff spit down the opening the branch had left in the center of the sagging grass without dislodging the toothpick from the corner of his mouth. The hole had spread at least two and a half feet around since I almost followed the branch down into it. I would have been impressed with his aim at this distance if I wasn't scared shitless. I knew we should have called the city instead of the pot-bellied, tobacco chewing, sorry excuse for a sheriff, but he was one of Betsy's old friends and she trusted him to know what to do.

She and the sheriff, Andrew Kulper, dated in high school over twenty-five years ago, before she and I got together. She always referred to him as an 'old friend' because she thought it bothered me if she brought up that they used to date. It didn't, but I let her think it did because it made me feel like I had some power over her despite how insignificant the issue.

The sheriff spit again, sending his loogie sailing down the center of the lawn-puncture once again, but made no move to call anyone, or even appear to be thinking about who to call. He seemed just fine with wasting time I knew we didn't have to waste, so I spoke up to move things along.

"We should probably get someone out here soon," I spouted. "Like real soon don't you think? We don't want this thing to get any bigger, right?"

Sheriff Andrew Kulper stared down through mirrored lenses into the widening depression, nodded his head, and emitted an ambiguous grunt. I couldn't tell if he was agreeing or disagreeing with me, and my patience with the officer and his nonchalant approach to the situation was nearing its end. When

19

Betsy asked him the question, he was suddenly able to use actual words to answer her.

"Andrew," she started, "will you be able to get someone out today? Reggie is . . . I mean Reggie and I are concerned that this could be dangerous. Reggie said he read about these kind of holes swallowing up people, cars, and even entire houses down in Florida."

"Well, that's Florida for ya." The sheriff turned away from the hole, pointing his bulbous gut in the direction of my wife. "I don't think Reggie needs to worry too much. Florida's nothin' but soft and sloppy swampland, it's no wonder things like this happen there. Probably just the first steps in the whole worthless state sinking down into the ocean. We got ourselves good, solid Texas soil here."

He paused as if he was being reverent just for mentioning the word 'Texas'. Then, he turned his head toward the hole and spit into it again, but not before flashing an awkward, half-smile at Betsy; the toothpick still cocked off to the side of his mouth like a permanent fixture. Under normal circumstances the entire interaction would have sent me into a blood-boiled frenzy, but there was no time for that now. He could pine over my wife all he wanted, hell; he could take her. All I cared about presently was not being eaten by a hole in my backyard.

"So, you *will* have someone out today, right?" I asked.

The sheriff turned to face me now, his smile vanishing along the way, transforming into a scowl. The angle of his toothpick enhanced the disdain radiating from his expression.

"Andrew said he would, Reggie," Betsy chimed in, perhaps sensing the tension building between the sheriff and myself.

"No he didn't," I said, feeling my usual urge to argue with Betsy being redirected at Sheriff Kulper. I maintained what I assumed was eye contact with the man, staring into the center of his mirrored lenses as I continued. "He said *I* didn't have anything to worry about, but he did not say he would send someone from the city today. So, will there be someone here today, Sheriff?"

Betsy flinched in reaction, but her protest stopped short of her throat, most likely out of surprise from not being the one my aggression was pointed at. I regretted taking that tone with the sheriff, but only because I knew it could create a situation counterproductive to having the sinkhole fixed. He flashed a quick smile at me, but not in the same way he smiled at Betsy.

This smile was sly, and subtle, and said *I've been inside your wife, and if you're not careful I'll be in there again.* I don't know why he was still hung up on a woman he dated over twenty years ago. What the sheriff didn't realize was, I did him a huge favor by ending up with Betsy, because he didn't have the gumption or wherewithal to handle a banshee like her.

The poor, love-sick sap had no idea that if I let him leave with Betsy right this second, he'd be sucking on the business end of the pistol that hung on his hip by the end of the week. Betsy just had that effect on people who weren't practiced in her ways like I was, but I've been training for years. The sheriff swiveled his head over from me back to Betsy, adjusting his smile along the way to one of pathos, and unrequited love.

"I'll call over to the city offices from my car, and have someone out here within a few hours to take a look, Betsy," he said, doing his best to add a comforting element to the tone of his voice, but instead he sounded like a pubescent teenager telling the girl he liked that he would gladly do her homework for her.

"Thank you, Andrew," she said, smiling with gratitude before turning to me. "See, Reggie? Andrew is taking care of it."

"Well, thank you very much, *Andrew,*" I said, unable to keep the derision from my tone.

I turned on my heel and walked purposefully to the back door and through it, leaving Betsy to walk the lovesick sheriff to his cruiser. I went into the kitchen and immediately began to make a pot of coffee. Even if someone from the city came out tonight, I couldn't imagine this being a quick job, and it was already too late in the day for a crew to get a good start.

The best I could hope for would be if someone actually did come out from the city, *and* they halfway knew a thing or two about what we're dealing with. At least then I could get some peace of mind from someone who would actually know if my overreaction was, or was not, warranted. Worst case, no one came because the sheriff did not alert anyone out of spite, and I sat in the kitchen watching a hole creep closer and closer to the house. Either way, I was not sleeping tonight.

5

The goddamn edges of the thing had already pushed out an extra foot since the morning. If I were any good at calculations, I would've been able to track how much the sinkhole would grow per hour. I imagined I would have to use some kind of chart or graph, but I'm not too good with those either.

I watched the first drip of coffee pass through the filter and land at the bottom of the pot, evaporating in a soft hiss. Close behind the initial drip comes the steady stream flowing hot, black, and thick. I liked my coffee strong, and since Betsy hated it that way I would have the pot to myself.

I knew I couldn't just sit and watch the hole, so I decided to dedicate the rest of my afternoon and evening to finding out as much about sinkholes as I could. For that, I would need to use the computer, which might be an issue if Betsy already had plans for it. We only had the one computer, and Betsy insisted it be in the living room.

The computer was older, and bigger, and looked terrible next to the ottoman, but she'd worn me down like always. I barely used the thing, but she spent hours on it learning how to build new monstrosities for that damn cat. I usually didn't mind her going down those rabbit holes, and staying glued to the thing for hours, because it gave me time to myself. The only drawback was Betsy would not relinquish control of the computer if she was using it, and guarded it like a mother bear her cubs. I did not look forward to trying to convince her I needed the computer more than her, especially since I rarely touched it.

I heard the front door close and I snapped from my train of thought, waiting for Betsy to come into the kitchen to give me nine kinds of hell for how I spoke to *Andrew*. I stood in front of the coffee maker with my hands on the countertop, readying myself to put on a show. As much as I didn't give two shits in a sack about respecting the local law enforcement, especially when they clearly pined for my wife, I could not get into another argument with Betsy.

I was going to need to agree with her and apologize almost immediately so as to not waste any precious research time. I glanced out the window into the backyard. The sun had already made half of its descent into the west, and I swore the sinkhole looked like it had already grown in the few minutes since we'd all been out there. The other reason to keep from falling into a debate with Betsy was the computer. I needed to use it, and I knew she wasn't above keeping me off it just to spite me for disagreeing with her.

Betsy's footsteps padded toward the kitchen. I had my apology pre-loaded and ready to spring from my mouth as soon as she stepped in. I'd never tried a pre-emptive apology with her before, but I thought it might take her by surprise enough to kill the argument before it was able to manifest. The footsteps slowed, then stopped, and I turned to face her, only to see she hadn't come in yet.

I waited a few seconds, then a few seconds more, bracing myself for the storm that didn't come. I slowly walked across the kitchen, still half-expecting Betsy to fly around the corner on fire with rage, but I made it to the doorway unscathed.

I peeked around the wall to see Betsy with her back to me, busily fussing with her never-ending cat-house project. Sandman was napping on the windowsill and opened his eyes when he sensed me enter the room. His bright yellow eyes shone heavy with disdain, which was fine by me since the feeling was mutual. It was a mutual understanding of a mutual hate. Betsy was humming to herself as she worked, and didn't notice I was behind her until I spoke up.

"So," I started. "He really is sending someone tonight, right?"

24

"He said he was," she said, matter-of-fact without breaking from her work. "But also, like he said, I don't think we need to worry too much about it."

She went back to humming, still not turning from the important job of cat-house remodeling. I could feel my face go hot and flushed, and my blood pressure shot up so high so quickly I thought I might pass out. I couldn't afford to blow my top, though, at least not at the moment. As much as I knew the sheriff's remarks to Betsy were said to emasculate me, and make me seem like a foolish worrywart in front of my wife, I had to let it go. Besides, that beer-bellied idiot didn't know shit from Shinola, and couldn't catch his own ass in the act of a wet fart without GPS *and* a road map. I wouldn't be taking advice on what I should or shouldn't worry about from an ass-hat like him. I took a slow, deep breath and exhaled carefully without making any noise.

"You know, I'm sure he's probably right." Each word felt like passing razors through my esophagus to get them out, and in the correct order. "If anybody knew if I should be worried or not it would be him. I'm sure he'll have someone from the city over here to tell us all is well in no time."

Betsy paused and turned from the new layer of carpet she was applying to a section of Sandman's palace. I must have laid it on too thick, and she'd figured out I was up to something. I quickly knitted my facial features together to look as non-confrontational as possible, and was even able to force a weak smile. I braced myself again for a tidal wave of verbal assault, but was again surprised to be met with softened, still waters.

"See," she said, smiling and without mumbling, "there's no use in getting all worked up over some hole that's not a real hole anyway. I'm glad Andrew was able to get through to you."

She nodded, continued smiling, and turned back to her cat carpeting. I'm glad she did too, because my face was no longer able to disguise the disgust I felt over having to pretend an oafish dolt like Sheriff Kulper would actually be able to 'get through' to me. Sandman eyed me from the sill with a look that said he knew I was full of shit.

"Do I smell coffee you're making in there, Reggie?" Betsy asked, still focused on making the small square of carpet fit perfectly.

"You sure do," I spouted. "You want a cup?"

I forgot I'd made it extra strong on purpose to avoid having to share, but at this point I didn't want to do anything to poke the bear, so to speak.

"I'd love a cup," she said. "Thank you dear."

I slipped back into the kitchen for the coffee, and to refocus myself. Betsy's uncharacteristic behavior had temporarily thrown me off. I turned on the faucet in the sink and waited for the water to get warm. I tried to keep myself from looking out into the yard, but couldn't help it and snuck a peek. I immediately wished I hadn't.

The sinkhole had clearly gotten bigger by several inches. When the water was warm enough I pulled a mug down from the cabinet and filled it a little more than halfway. Then, I topped it off with the black death I'd brewed, hoping I'd diluted it enough for Betsy to find palatable. I pulled down a second large mug, and filled it to the brim straight from the steaming hot carafe. I'd already wasted enough time. I needed to get to the computer and find out how to fix this thing, and I needed to do it fast.

I hurried from the kitchen with a mug of hot coffee in each hand, trying my best not to spill. I walked through the next room, stopping for only a moment to drop Betsy's coffee off to her. setting it on the table she kept next to the cat-house. It was covered in carpet squares, glue, and a box of headless finishing nails.

"Here you go hon," I said, doing my best impression of a chipper person. "Enjoy."

I continued to the living room, hoping not to be called back or questioned about what I was up to. Thankfully, Betsy simply mumbled what I assumed was a 'thanks,' and kept right on working. I approached the computer in the corner of the

26

room, and carefully pulled the chair out from the desk, trying hard not to make a sound.

Even though Betsy wasn't currently using the computer I was still worried she'd suddenly realize she needed it, putting an end to my research before it could even begin. I sat on the chair Betsy had bought from a resale shop, and the springs in the cushioned top groaned the squeaky wail of old age. I pulled myself up to the computer, took a large sip of the hot, black coffee, burning my tongue in the process, and moved the mouse around to rouse the dinosaur of a PC out of sleep mode.

A picture of two kittens dressed up to look like nineteen twenties era gangsters were posed standing in front of a backdrop of an old-style 'social club' from the same time period. There were small, plastic tommy-guns strapped to each kitten's back. Betsy was always changing the wallpaper of the computer's desktop, and it was always a picture of kittens anthropomorphized as some 'cutesy' character.

I hadn't seen this one before, but they were all the same to me. I sipped my coffee while the computer buzzed, hummed, and creaked through whatever processes it needed to run before being ready for use. The thing was so old it may as well have had a crank on the back to start it up. I couldn't imagine it had too many more miles left on it. All I needed was a few more hours though, and then the thing could go to hell for all I cared.

When the computer was finally ready for use, I double clicked on the multi-colored, planet-looking icon that opened the Internet. The screen became filled with pictures of kittens with text laid on top, but I didn't bother reading what any of it said.

I'm sure it was one of the many websites Betsy read regularly that told her how much more important her cat was than her husband. Like I said, I didn't know much about computers, but I knew how to use a search engine and typed the address into the bar at the top of the page. The dust-covered relic of a machine whined, clicked, and hummed, seeming to be in pain while the page loaded. I took a long sip of my coffee, which was now at a more suitable drinking temperature, cracked my knuckles, and typed the word 'sinkhole.'

I initially started my research by trying to find 'how to fix a sinkhole,' but after around thirty minutes of reading repair methods from do-it-yourselfers all over the world, I realized I needed to jump back some. All of the methods for fixing a sinkhole were contingent upon what actually caused the thing to form in the first place. I adjusted my search parameters to 'what causes a sinkhole,' and a few clicks later I was on my way to becoming the foremost leading expert on the subject.

Well, at least the foremost leading expert on what caused sinkholes in this county, but still I sucked in the information like a broke whore working a glory hole. The researching of the now revised subject matter opened another *hole* of information collecting that I fell into, not realizing how deep it went.

It turns out there were several different ways a sinkhole could happen, which added an additional layer of information for me to peel away. They could be caused by something buried in the ground that fails, breaks, or collapses, such as sewer lines, different types of pipes, septic tanks, and even an improperly completed past excavation.

I read one cause could often be from continuous heavy rain pushing and moving sections of loosely packed dirt just beneath the surface layer. That usually happened when said dirt lacked clay and other binding elements to solidify the soil. According to a few of the sites I visited, those types of sinkholes could be safely, and semi-easily, fixed with a shovel, some concrete, and densely packed soil that included an abundance of clay. The fix seemed easy and straightforward, but the problem was, after all my reading, I didn't think our sinkhole qualified for that particular category.

It turned out the 'easy to fix' sinkholes usually topped out at around a three foot diameter, and the one in my backyard was already well beyond that. I hadn't bothered to check on the hole since I sat down at the computer, and I shuddered to think how much it might have spread in that time.

According to what I read, my worrying was completely justified, because it looked like our sinkhole qualified as the kind that swallows cars, people, and yes, entire houses. The cause of these sinkholes was usually from a shift in the earth that produced some kind of hollow chasm or pit. Even more unsettling was the possibility of it being a pre-existing gash in the earth that had opened, and had since been covered up. This information was particularly alarming, since I would expect a city official, such as a sheriff, to know about a said pre-existing matter, and pass the information on to those who may be affected.

I pictured Sheriff Kulper's smug face staring me down while telling Betsy there was nothing to be worried about, all the while knowing there certainly was. I imagined the wheels turning in his Cro-Magnon-like skull as he insultingly placated my fear while having a selfish ulterior motive. I was sure he hoped by telling me it was nothing to worry about, I'd end up messing with the thing until the ground opened up and took me away.

With me out of the way he'd be free and clear to intensify his advances on Betsy, reminding her of old times together so he could swoop in and take my place. My anger seethed at the thought of such treachery, and I wished for a moment I could go back in time a few hours and push the fat, incompetent sheriff right into the sinkhole. This only lasted a minute or two, and I made myself calm down, knowing the emotion was counterproductive at this point.

It was well after five now, and no city office would be open to call and query whether or not official records showed a known depression had existed on the property at some point. I half-wished I'd found out the house was built on an Indian burial ground, because I could deal with poltergeists turning chairs over and moving things across the counter. Hell, it would probably make things a little more fun and interesting around here, and while it might be an inconvenience, it wouldn't worse than having the entire house drop into the ground.

When I'd collected enough data on sinkholes themselves, I had to switch gears and begin researching the history of my property. If something like this happened years ago and had since been repaired, there would have to be some kind of record of it somewhere.

I wasn't sure exactly how to go about finding such information, so I started by typing our address into the search engine just to see what results would show up. There were pages that showed it on a map, or asked me if I needed directions to or away from the address. There were old, outdated listings from when the house was on the market well before we bought it, as well as accompanying photos of the interior and the yard.

I meticulously scoured every photo of the backyard I could find, searching for any sign of something different that might lead me to an answer, but I could tell no difference. I started specifically looking for the history of the property going back as far as I could to see if any kind of disaster, natural or otherwise, might have happened in our town, either directly or indirectly involving the property that I now owned.

I could find no record of any earthquakes in the area, which I'd learned from my earlier research were responsible for hollowing out these underground chasms that went on to become sinkholes. This tiny bit of info gave me little solace, since earthquakes didn't really ever happen in Texas, but it was something to cross of the list and move on from.

Poring through old newspaper articles as well as any town records that were accessible online showed many of what were called 'disasters,' but were mostly just a handful of bad storms with heavy rain. I don't know what else I expected to find, what with this being east Texas and all. It either rained to the point of catastrophic flooding, or didn't to the point of

causing a catastrophic drought. Outside of those two extremes, I couldn't find anything that stood out and grabbed my attention … until a few clicks later when I did.

7

I followed several links until I came to a story about a real motherfuck of a storm that rolled through these parts fifty-two years ago. The story was solely about the damage and destruction in our town, but the article was from a newspaper two towns and over a hundred miles away. After skimming through a few other articles from the same paper, I found the reason.

It seemed our town was left in such a state of disaster the local paper had to shut down for two weeks to repair damages to the building and equipment. Therefore, all of the news pertaining to the storm was printed in papers from the surrounding towns with significantly less damage. When the local paper resumed operations, there were no articles about the storm or the damage to the town published in any subsequent issues. My guess was the townsfolk who lived through it had no desire to read about it, so the paper went about like nothing ever happened.

A few searches later I was able to find several articles on the storm from the other towns' papers, and I left them open in individual windows so I could easily reference between them. It took another two hours and three more cups of coffee, but I was able to piece together what the cause of my sinkhole was, and another reason why the local paper might have decided not to write about the storm.

According to the articles, the reason the storm was so particularly devastating was due to the several tornadoes it spawned all at the same time. Reports were sketchy and speculative at best regarding the actual number, but the consensus was there were more than five and less than twelve.

The margin of error was on the larger side, but there was no accounting for people who saw the same tornado in a different spot and double counted. Still, the town itself wasn't very large, and I couldn't imagine the damage two tornadoes at the same time would do, let alone five or more.

The power and intensity of the tornadoes was so strong there were reports of them digging through the ground as they traveled across town like there were giant drill-bits attached to the bottom of them. Another paper reported our town buying a record twenty tons of dirt that was loaded into dump trucks, shuttled back and forth, and used to fill gouges in the ground left by the flock of tornadoes.

The article talked about how a discount had been given partly out of sympathy, but mostly because a third of the dirt supplied was composed of sand and gravel. It was reasoned that once it was all mixed together it wouldn't cause any problems. The whole thing sounded like a bum deal to me, but I guess they were desperate enough to take the risk.

There was one other piece of news regarding the storm reported in three of the papers I was looking through, and while vague, there were several details that remained constant. Apparently the storm came on a lot faster than predicted, and no one foresaw the tornadoes that would accompany it. The schools shut down early, but they couldn't get all of the kids home before they were already in the thick of it.

Each article talked about one bus filled with children being picked up off of the road and carried away by one of the tornadoes. There were witnesses as far as twenty miles away who reported seeing it crash face down into the earth like a giant cigarette being snubbed out in the bottom of a filthy bar ashtray.

The bus didn't explode on impact or twist down in on itself like a meat grinder made especially for children. The bus went deep into one of the massive gorges the murder of tornadoes had dug into the ground. There were a handful of closer witnesses who watched the bus plunge beneath the surface like it was taking the fast lane straight to Hell.

After the storm had blown over, the police investigated the reported area, but as they stood at the edge of the newly gouged earth, they saw no bus in the ground. They walked that particular crevasse end to end twice, finding no sign of where it was claimed the bus should have been. The police were far too busy to waste time looking for a bus that probably wasn't there.

The bus and children were missing, that much was known, but there were other witness accounts claiming to have seen a bus washed off the road. The bus was never found, nor where the bodies of the children or driver, but with so many casualties of the storm they just got lost in the shuffle. The bus being washed off the road and down river made more sense to the police, so that was the story they decided to go with. I could find no follow up to this story in further editions of those, or any other papers.

There was one consistent similarity through all three articles in the form of a photograph. It was taken from the perspective of someone standing behind two police officers and three of the men who claimed to see the bus fall from the sky. They were all standing at the edge of a big fucking hole in the ground.

One of the men is pointing down into it. One man is scratching his head, and one of the police officers has his hands on his hips. I noticed it right away, which was probably why I got so cold so fast, and had a sudden and intense need to empty my bowels. The edges of my vision started to blur, so I shut my eyes and rubbed them vigorously with my thumb and forefinger. I opened my eyes and the picture came into focus, giving me final confirmation. The three men and the two police officers were standing in my backyard.

I'm not sure how long I'd been staring at the photograph when Betsy snapped me out of my trance. I'd enlarged the photo so I could pore over every detail, and it filled the entire screen. It had been taken well before digital or high-definition technology was available or even thought of, but despite the primitive medium I was still able to glean some interesting information from it.

One detail in particular that hijacked my train of thought was the actual width of the opening cleaved into the ground by the twister. It wasn't as wide across as my imagination made it out to be when I was reading the articles. Instead of the vast crater I had convinced myself existed, the gorge the men stood in front of couldn't have been more than ten feet wide. Like I said before, I'm awful at judging distance, but at least looking at the picture I had a decent perspective based on the other elements shown. Sure, the rift itself was miles long, but wasn't wide enough for a long jumper with a good head start to have any trouble leaping across.

This gave me some hope, but it was snuffed out almost the moment it began to blossom. At first, I thought if the width of the hole was only ten feet, I wouldn't have to worry about the sinkhole reaching the house, and I might even be able to mark off a safety perimeter to make the eventual filling of the hole easier.

What stole this glimmer of hope was the realization that I couldn't see down into the small canyon. Sure, I had a clear view of the width, but that was all the angle of the photo allowed me to see. For all I knew the ground beneath could be hollowed out for god knows how far in both directions.

If an entire school bus had indeed taken a nosedive into this chasm, and after the fact could not be seen from the surface, then the hole had to be more far-reaching in all directions than I'd first imagined. There was no way to gauge how many feet of rain water had rushed down into the gorge, working to carve away the dirt around it in order to push itself deeper and deeper into the earth.

For all I knew the house was already compromised, and seconds from dropping from view of the surface. When Betsy put her hand down on my shoulder, I snapped from my doom-filled daze, and spilled the cup of coffee I'd held hovering at my lips for who knows how long.

"Reggie," she crowed, "what are you sleepin' or something? I've been calling you for the last five goddamn minutes!"

The coffee was no longer hot, so it didn't burn, but was still uncomfortable and inconvenient to have in my lap. Having nothing handy to wipe it with, I rubbed the stale, cold coffee into my jeans, hoping to spread it out enough to make the moistness not completely unbearable. The way Betsy snapped let me know the minor reprieve of cooperative patience was no longer in effect.

"No, I wasn't sleepin'!" I barked out of habit, but quickly pulled back. "I was . . . I was just zoned out I guess."

Betsy huffed a grunt of impatient annoyance at having to be pulled from her task to walk the ten feet to come get me.

"Well, I was tryin' to tell you Andrew called." Her voice softened at mention of the sheriff by first name, although was still not completely free of its usual venom.

"When?" I asked confused. "When did he call? I didn't hear the phone ring? Did he say when the city was coming? Did he say anything about a sto-"

"Jesus, Reggie slow down!" She half-shrieked, cutting me off. "I was on the phone talking to my sister, and I clicked over to him on the call waiting."

This made sense, since Betsy would often be on the phone with her sister for hours, but rarely did she ever click over if another call was coming in unless she was expecting her mother to call. It made me wonder if she was being entirely truthful with me. Had she been the one to call Kulper?

If so, had she called to inquire about the sinkhole, or was their conversation more devious and deceptive in nature? I shook these thoughts from my mind before they distracted me further. I had more important things to worry about now than the imaginary infidelities of Betsy.

"He said the city can't come out tonight," she continued. "Said they'd be out first thing in the morning."

"First thing? What time is that?"

"I don't know." She shrugged, turning to head back to the other room. "I think he said ten or so."

I held back the kind of reaction I was typically prone to when receiving news that was less than what I desired, which was a surprise to us both. She was halfway lingering in the doorway, waiting to react to an explosion of anger that didn't come. I was angry, there was no doubt about that, but I'd already predicted something like this from the sheriff, so it wasn't like I didn't see it coming. Plus, my mind was far too preoccupied to dedicate energy to being angry at something I saw coming a mile away.

"Oh . . .uh, okay then," I managed, sounding as meek as I could. "I guess . . . I guess that'll be fine."

Betsy paused, turned to me, and opened her mouth to say something, but changed her mind before the words could escape.

"Okay then," she finally said, turning to go back to her cat-doings. "Don't stay on that thing too long. You'll strain your eyes, and besides I'm gonna' need to get on there pretty soon myself."

"I'm just wrapping up now," I said to her back as she exited.

I had all the information I could stomach at the moment anyway, so I didn't see the benefit in pressing the issue with her

38

to maintain control of the paperweight we called a computer. The city wasn't coming out tonight, but I'd figured that all along, and who knew when or even if they'd come tomorrow. I was going to have to handle this on my own.

I stood at the kitchen window, staring into the darkness with a death-grip on the handle of a cup of coffee I poured ten minutes ago, but had yet to drink from. The light over the backdoor didn't cast much illumination past ten feet or so, but I didn't need it to see that the perimeter of the sinkhole had spread.

I didn't realize how much time I'd spent on the computer, and thought I'd have more daylight to work with. We were edging out of summer, but not so far from it that the days would be getting shorter already. Still, here I was looking at a night sky I swore had come more than thirty minutes earlier than it had twenty-four hours ago.

"Reggie, are you staring out at that hole again?"

I jumped, dropping the full mug of coffee into the sink. It shattered, spraying lukewarm coffee and ceramic shards up into my face. I could normally hear Betsy coming, but I had been too deep in thought to be aware of my surroundings. I turned around to face her, wiping coffee from my eyes on the backs of my hands.

"Andrew is sending someone tomorrow. There's nothing you can do until then, and staring at it ain't gonna' do a thing. And I hope that wasn't one of my good mugs!"

My eyes cleared and I could now see the glare I'd only been able to feel moments ago. She was clutching Sandman at her side, and the cat stared me down as well, matching the intensity of its master. I took a deep breath, struggling to suppress my boiling rage, because I couldn't explode on her just yet. She'd never believe the conclusions I'd drawn based on the articles I read, and she'd be right to. Hell, I hardly wanted to believe it myself.

40

"Sorry about that hon," I said slowly. "I wasn't looking at the hole, I was just daydreaming."

"It's too dark out to be daydreaming," she barked as she turned to leave. "And clean up your damn mess."

"I was wondering that actually. Didn't it stay lighter out for longer yester-"

Betsy was already in the other room before I could finish, and she either didn't hear or was ignoring me. I turned back to the window, taking another long look at the sinkhole to make sure it hadn't grown any more while my back was turned. Satisfied, but not entirely convinced, I started picking chunks of the broken mug out of the sink, and tossed them into the trash can in the cabinet below.

"I hope you're putting those pieces of broken glass in a paper bag before you put them in the trash," Betsy snarled from the other room.

I spun around to make sure she wasn't behind me again before calling back to her.

"I am, I am," I mumbled, turning back to the sink.

That was when I saw something, or at least I thought I did. I stuck my face as close to the window as possible to make sure I wasn't being fooled by a glare off the glass. I didn't see it anymore, but I couldn't convince myself it was in my head either. For a split second I saw a pale yellow light coming up from the center of the sinkhole.

Shortly after I saw, or thought I saw, light coming out of the hole, I grabbed a flashlight from the utility drawer, the expensive one that was supposedly used by police and elite special forces, and tried to slip out the backdoor to take a look. I'd barely taken one step outside when Betsy's screech halted me in my tracks.

She heard the squeak of the hinges when I opened the door, and flew into the kitchen brandishing a hammer. I realized the hammer was meant for working on the cat-house rather than throttling me, but I knew it wouldn't be out of the question for her to give the tool a dual usage.

"Reggie, you get back in this house this instant!" Betsy hollered as she entered the kitchen. "I told you to stop worrying about that thing, and let the people who know what they're doing handle it tomorrow. The last thing I need is for you to fall into that hole, and I have to get the sheriff back out here with the fire department to save you."

I stepped back inside and shoved the flashlight into my back pocket, hoping she hadn't seen it.

"I was just checking on the-"

"You were just checking on nothing!" she snapped, cutting me off. "Stay out of the backyard until the city workers show up tomorrow. I mean it!"

Without giving me a chance to respond or challenge, Betsy turned and left the kitchen in a huff. I sat quietly at the kitchen table for a few minutes before getting up to rummage through the cabinet used for storing miscellaneous items such as WD-40, which was exactly what I was looking for. I took the can over to the door and liberally sprayed the lubricant on the three hinges before hopping back over to the cabinet to put the can away.

When I sat back down, I realized the smell of pressurized, synthetic grease hung heavy in the room around me. If I didn't do something about it, and quickly, Betsy would be able to smell it in the next room and figure out what I was up to.

I frantically scanned the kitchen for something to mask the WD-40 scent, but my options were limited. My first thought was to make more coffee, but I was afraid it would take too long for the aroma to cover the telltale grease smell. I could think of only one other option, and leapt toward the cabinet under the sink.

I yanked it open and grabbed out the plastic bucket Betsy stored there, along with the bottle of pine-scented floor cleaner. I placed the bucket in the sink, started running water into it, and dumped a liberal amount of the cleaner in as well. My eyes burned as the harsh chemical cleanser fumes rose from the bucket, but it was worth the pain. Within seconds the kitchen smelled like a thousand concentrated cab air-fresheners.

When the bucket was two thirds full, I turned off the water, looked up, and caught another glimpse of the yellow light coming up from the sinkhole. I knew I had definitely seen it this time, and there was no denying it. I heard something behind me and spun around, terrified and ready to strike. It was Betsy, with a confused look on her face that at any moment could slip into anger again.

"Reggie," she started, "what in the hell are you doing now?"

"Oh, well uh," I sputtered, trying to regain my composure. "I thought giving the kitchen a good deep clean would be just the thing to keep my mind off the backyard, and tire me out good so I fall asleep without any problems."

Betsy narrowed her eyes, unable to make sense of what I was saying, but also finding no reason to not believe me. She cocked her head and sniffed at the air, scrunching her nose in a way that that said she wasn't enjoying what she smelled. For a

43

moment I thought she could smell the WD-40 through the heavy pine-scented cover, and I wracked my brain for an excuse if indeed this was the case.

"You used way too much of that shit," she said, pinching her nose and pointing at the pine cleaner I'd left on the counter. "Open the window before you make yourself sick."

I nodded, trying to look agreeable without rousing any further suspicion. Betsy turned to leave the kitchen but paused, and looked over her shoulder at me.

"I'm gonna be on the front porch. I have to spray paint some pieces of the new wing I'm adding onto to Sandman's house, so I'll be out there if you need me. Huffing paint fumes is way better than breathing this pine shit. I feel like my lungs are on fire."

Betsy left the kitchen, and I heard her fumbling in the other room with whatever she was taking out front to paint. I should've helped her, but I felt the kind gesture would make me look suspicious so I stood still and waited.

"Don't forget to open the dang window, Reggie," she shouted from the front door. "I don't want to come back in and find you passed out on the floor from pine fumes!"

I would have called back 'yes dear,' but the door slammed before I had the chance. I crossed to the window over the sink, reached out to push it open, and froze as my fingers touched the pane. The light was back again, shining up from the hole, but now it was slowly flashing on and off like the signs on the road indicating construction was up ahead, or even like a turn signal on a vehicle.

I jumped back from the window, feeling lightheaded, and leaned against the table for stability. I'd never fainted before in my life, but I imagined this was what it felt like just before you did. There was a coldness that started at my feet and slowly climbed up my body like a slinky in reverse. The feeling of doom and despair settled over me again, pushing down so heavy on my chest it became difficult to breathe.

I stepped up to the window again and watched as the center of the sinkhole collapsed inward, making the transformation from curious indention to full blown hole. The flashing light made it easier for me to see the ground fall away as the hole spread to within a foot of the ever-widening border.

Dirt clouds rose slowly and looked extra eerie with the flashing yellow light illuminating the particles to make a translucent haze. As the dust settled, I saw motion on the far edge of the hole. It was hard to tell what it was through the settling dirt and flashing light, so I put my face up to the glass of the window and squinted to get a better look.

I hoped my mind was playing tricks on me, and what I thought I saw wasn't really there. The flashing light stopped suddenly, and the hole was plunged back into darkness. No matter how hard I tried to convince myself I was wrong, I knew I wasn't. What I'd seen on the back end of the hole was a tiny, bone-white hand clutching the newly formed edge. Then the electricity cut off, filling the house with the same blackness that filled the hole.

11

I held the good flashlight in my hand again. ready to dash out into the backyard, but unsure what I was going to do once I got out there. At this point it seemed all I was prepared to do was run to the edge of the hole and shine a light down into it, which wasn't exactly productive, but better than nothing. Before I could reach for the backdoor, Betsy appeared behind me in the kitchen again.

"Reggie, what did you do to the lights?" Her tone was accusatory and laced with annoyance.

"Nothing," I replied. "I was just standing here cleaning."

"Well, I'm in the middle of painting," she snapped, snatching the flashlight from my hand. "I need this to see what the hell I'm doing out there. If you want to clean in the dark, then light a candle."

She flicked the flashlight on and the powerful beam illuminated a path in front of her out of the kitchen. Betsy got to the doorway, stopped, and turned back to me.

"And open that dang window, Reggie! You're gonna' give yourself brain damage if you haven't already!"

The light grew dimmer the farther away she got, and when the front door slammed I was left alone in darkness once again. I dove for the utility drawer at the end of the counter, and yanked it open hard enough to pull it all the way out. The back end of the drawer tipped down when it slid free, and the contents clattered to the ground.

The sound was deafening against the backdrop of a still, dark house, and I froze, still clutching the handle of the drawer, waiting for Betsy to rush in and scold me for my clumsiness. After ten seconds I exhaled, satisfied the noise didn't carry out to the front porch. I crouched over the spilled contents, placed the

46

empty drawer next to the pile, and used both hands to rummage through the pile of junk.

There was a rubber-band ball as well as what felt like hundreds of loose rubber-bands tangled up with various sizes of paperclips, and twist-ties. My fingers passed across three tubes of Chapstick all in various stages of use, as well as an innumerable amount of loose batteries ranging from AAA to D. I pushed them to the side and several rolled off to low-lying areas of the kitchen floor.

I sifted through a thick, uneven stack of coupons and receipts, and pricked my finger on a plastic baggie filled with thumbtacks. I cursed Betsy for storing them that way, but remembered it was I who'd actually stowed them last. Finally, my hand landed on what I was looking for hidden amongst the batteries that hadn't rolled away.

It was a short, thin flashlight I'd bought off the impulse rack at the hardware store months ago. It was camouflaged, but that didn't matter as much to me now as it did when I initially bought it. I felt for the rubber button on the backend, pushed it in, and prayed the thing still worked. A bright, crisp LED beam of light blasted from the lens of the tiny thing, and I silently rejoiced.

I pushed the button again to kill the light, gathered as much of the spilled contents I could hold between my hands and forearms, and dropped them back into the drawer. I stood up, thrust the drawer back into the counter, and kicked away the stray items that didn't make it back in the drawer. I'd have to deal with that later.

I bounded for the back door in three long strides, grabbed the knob, and opened the door slowly. The hinges spun without a sound now, not that it mattered since Betsy was outside, but at least it was one less thing to worry about later. When I stepped out onto the lawn, the freshly greased door closed on its own behind me.

The air outside was still, and heavy with East Texas humidity, but laced with a stale rank I couldn't put my finger on.

The feeling of dread flooded my sensory receptors again, and I strained my eyes to look across the backyard for any sign of movement, but there was none. Even the blades of grass stood statuesque with no breeze for them to bow to.

For a moment I thought I'd become frozen in time. I didn't realize I'd stopped breathing until a loud clatter rang out from the fence to my left. I gulped down a lungful of air and spun toward the sound, pressing the button on the flashlight as I did. I aimed the beam of light in the direction the sound came from, and caught the tail end of the shadow of something going over the fence.

It wasn't out of the ordinary for possums, raccoons, or other cats besides Sandman to walk along the fence. Any other day this would have been a reasonable explanation for what I saw, and one I would willingly accept without a second thought. Not today though. Not when there was a ten-foot wide hole in my backyard. Not after I read about that bus.

The next few things happened quickly, too quickly. I heard another distinct clatter from the fence again, but this time to my right. It was immediately followed by an inhuman screech from the direction of the hole, followed by more banging against the fence, but this time from both sides at once.

I swiveled on my heels, shining the light erratically in all directions but only succeeding in catching glimpses of shadows all around me. Then, just as abruptly as the chaos started, it ended, leaving me in the still silence again, but now I knew I wasn't alone anymore.

I was planted in place, unable to move if I wanted to, like concrete roots had sprung from the bottoms of my feet cementing me permanently to this spot. My thin beam of light landed back on the hole and danced around the perimeter in my less-than-steady hand as I waited. I wasn't sure for what, but I anticipated the worst. I was sure it was only a matter of seconds before the shadows I'd been chasing closed in to finish me off for witnessing their escape.

Nothing happened and the darkness fell heavy and silent around me, constrictive and smothering. I didn't realize I had moved until I found myself a foot away from the edge of the hole.

12

I stopped short and stumbled from the abrupt change in momentum. The small amount of light from the flashlight flickered, and then died completely. I smacked it on the side with the palm of my hand while it sputtered its last breaths of life in the form of a few dim flashes. I unscrewed the small cap off the end and spun the batteries, hoping my touch was all they needed to be resurrected, but when I returned the cap and pressed the button, nothing happened.

Then, the light from the hole started flashing again. It was brighter now, but only because I was closer. The last time the lights were flashing, the noise I heard around me suggested something had escaped the hole. If this were about to happen again, I wanted to see it coming. And if I was about to die, I had to see what was in that hole before I went.

I stepped up to the edge before the pale yellow light could hypnotize me into changing my mind and propel me back to the house. I looked down into the hole, trying to make sense of what I was seeing during the short bursts of light. The light was coming from two small, round discs about three or so feet apart. They didn't flash together in unison, and instead took turns, one lighting up as the other faded to black.

The light looked about twenty-five or thirty feet down, but I was no one to judge, and the swirling clouds of dirt obscured what the discs were attached to. I took another look around the backyard, paying special attention to where I'd heard the noise coming from the fence. The night was still and silent around me, but that did nothing to ease the dread currently squeezing my bowels with the grip of an inept snake handler.

I slowly bent down, got on my knees, and clutched clumps of grass at my sides, as if it were able to provide me with any safety. I brought my face down and peered over the edge, squinting hard to see through the dusty haze at the bottom.

Either the dust had settled enough, or I happened to be at just the right angle, but I was able to make out some black markings between the flashing circles of light. At first it looked like black lines arranged in no particular way, and against my better judgment I pushed my head below the edge, holding onto the patches of grass for dear life. Suddenly the markings didn't look so random.

They started to come together to form letters, and those letters formed words, and I could finally see it clearly. The letters between the flashing lights said School Bus. The entire back end of it came into focus like a magic-eye painting, which meant the front side was indeed facing down.

The emergency door on the back of the bus, the one I remember as a child teachers and bus drivers telling students to never touch unless it was a dire situation, was hanging wide open. The opening into the bus seemed impossibly darker than the rest of the hole, and although my vision could not pierce beyond the black square, I couldn't shake the feeling something inside was staring back up at me.

My stomach lurched, and the air grew intolerably cold. A hair-raising scream rang out, shattering the silence into a million unlucky shards. I pulled my head out of the hole and the screaming became more intense and desperate by the second.

It was coming from the front porch.

13

I forced myself to stand on unsteady jelly legs, but face-planted into the ground after a step and a half. I got back up, found my balance, and ran back to the house unsure of whether I should go through, or go through the gate to get to Betsy and the porch. Going through the gate was a more direct path, but it was dark and something might be waiting to catch me off guard.

If I went through the house it would take a few extra seconds, but I would be able to grab something to use as a weapon against whatever was making Betsy scream. I chose going through the house; that way, I could arm myself and possibly mount a sneak attack if I burst out through the front door.

I knew I was running despite having no sensation in my legs. My mind reeled with images of ghoulish, undead children. This was normally not a conclusion I would jump to, but the circumstances required a complete change of mindset. I hit the back door and pushed, forgetting I needed to turn the knob first, but made it in on my second attempt. The darkness in the kitchen seemed far more chilling and treacherous after what I'd seen in the sinkhole, and I involuntarily shivered.

I bolted through the kitchen and into the next room where Betsy had been working on her cat-house project all day, but something tripped me up. I heard a squeal as I fell on my chest like I was sliding headfirst into second base. The impact knocked the wind out of me, and I struggled to both breathe and get up. I looked behind me to see I had tripped over Sandman, who glared at me, seemingly unfazed.

The cat hissed as I used one of Betsy's unfinished, cat-related projects to pull myself up. The fall cost me precious seconds, and I still hadn't fully recovered my breath as I plodded to the hall closet. The screaming had stopped, but I wasn't sure if that was a good or bad thing.

I opened the closet door and felt around until my hand landed on the Louisville Slugger I was looking for. Still gasping for breath, I lunged at the front door with my free hand, and tore the door open ready to swing for the fences at whatever or whoever was attacking my wife. The scene I so recklessly threw myself into was not at all what I expected.

I lowered the bat and confusedly stared at Betsy, who was on the porch with the sheriff. They both wore similar expressions like that of a child caught with his hand in the cookie jar. They were standing closer together than necessary for a normal conversation, and my mind reeled with scenarios I didn't have time to think about.

"Reggie," said Betsy as she stepped away from the Sheriff and toward me, "what are you doing with that bat?"

"I – heard - you - scream," I said, sucking in air between each word. "What the hell is he doing here?"

"Andrew stopped by to check on us," she said in a wavering voice.

"I . . . uh, just wanted to make sure the hole hadn't spread and swallowed up the two of you and your house," the sheriff said, pulling nervously on the brim of the signature Stetson.

"What . . ." I gasped, finally able to control my breath. "What was all the screaming for?"

"Oh, I was so wrapped up my project I didn't even realize he was here until he tapped my on the shoulder. He scared the daylights out of me!"

"Sorry about that again," the Sheriff said, looking past and not at me. "I'll have to remember to announce myself next time."

I didn't believe a word either of them said, especially since it looked like they were in a contest to have the worst poker face. Now was not the time to find out why he was really here, but I was *actually* glad he was. I'd have to put aside my disdain for the man for the time being until we figured out exactly what was going on with the bus, along with the children who had finally escaped the hell they'd been trapped in for years. It even sounded crazy to me in my own mind, so I could only guess what the sheriff would think.

"Sheriff," I started, trying not to sound too worked up, "I need to show you something in the backyard."

"You don't need to show him the hole again, Reggie." Betsy's tone was like that of a mother scolding her child. "They're coming to look at it in the morning, and I already told you to stop worrying about it."

"Betsy's right," the sheriff chimed in. "Ain't nothing I can do about it by taking another look. The city will have the crew out in the morning, and you can talk to them all about it."

"You don't understand," I said, my frustration now showing as it mounted. "The hole opened, and there's-"

But I never got the chance to explain.

Two small, alabaster hands reached from behind the Sheriff, and wrapped themselves around his neck. Tiny fingers dug easily into his neck, and tore it open, exposing the inside of a now useless esophagus that resembled an inside out bratwurst. Betsy saw my eyes widen and turned to see what I was looking at. She let loose another horrifying scream, but this time with good reason.

14

The sheriff's body fell like a marionette whose strings had just been cut, landing hard on his knees before toppling forward to reveal the thing responsible for his grisly demise. It resembled a child in stature, but its face was decidedly not childlike in any sense of the word. Its eyes were like slits, and more rectangular than round, revealing onyx orbs through the narrow opening.

The thing's nose was flattened down against its face, with the end turned up like a pig, or a bat, or like that of a badly decomposed body. Its mouth was drawn back in a snarl that stretched the width of its face like the smile on a jack-o-lantern, but void of whimsy.

Tattered remnants of clothing hung from its gaunt white frame, resembling what at one time were a flannel shirt and a pair of blue jeans. The entirety of its flesh was bone-white with the exception of the tiny hands now stained in the sheriff's blood. The crimson stood out brightly against the ultra-pale complexion of the small creature, to the extent that it looked fake. Surely real human blood wasn't this rich in hue, but here I was staring at proof it indeed was.

The fountain of blood spewing from the severed artery in the sheriff's neck waned to a slow dribble now, but it was everywhere. The porch was covered in what was more blood than I ever thought could fit inside of one person. Yet, here I was seeing it with my own two eyes.

From the moment the sheriff's body dropped, I felt like time had stopped, and I had stopped with it, unable to move if I wanted to. Now, as I watched the child-looking creature take a step up onto the back of the man it had just slain, I realized time had indeed not stopped, and while I wanted to react, fear had shackled me to the floor.

The thing looked from me to Betsy, then down at the sheriff's body beneath its feet. Betsy let loose another terror-wracked shriek loud enough to be heard for miles as the child-creature got off the sheriff, and turned him over using only one bone-thin hand. The sheriff weighed four to five times what this thing weighed, but it didn't struggle flipping the corpse.

It thrust its hand down into the sheriff's belly, and came out clutching a handful of pink worms slick with the man's inside juices. The thing was holding the small intestine and began to pull more and more of it out like a magician pulling a never-ending stream of scarves from his hat.

Betsy screamed again, and this time the thing did not ignore her. It dropped the innards like it was tired of the trick, leapt the entire length of the porch, and attached itself to Betsy's torso, wrapping its legs around her back. Her screams turned to choking, garbled gasps as the pint-sized monster wrapped its bloodstained hands around her neck. My knuckles ached as I realized I was squeezing the handle of the bat like I was trying to wring water from the wood. My feet broke from the bonds of fear, and I stepped toward Betsy, the bat held high over my head ready to strike.

She began to flail in an attempt to shake the thing from her, but it maintained a firm grasp. I wanted to bring the bat down on its head, but with all the movement and it being attached to Betsy I couldn't find my opening. If I started swinging at the monster there was absolutely no way I wouldn't hit Betsy.

Beads of blood sprayed across my face from the wounds in Betsy's neck where the thing had dug its fingers in. Betsy turned toward me, and while she could no longer speak, she pleaded with her eyes for me to help her. The blood flowed freely from the wounds in her neck, and I decided I needed to at least try. I cocked the bat back over my right shoulder, and

56

swung with all my might, hoping to connect with the creature's head.

I spun almost completely around and stumbled back into the wall, realizing I had missed completely. I recovered my balance and brought the bat back to strike again, but my arms wilted as the bat suddenly felt like a lead weight in my hands. The creature was standing next to the quivering, convulsing body of my wife, holding her head in its hands, having ripped it from her body. Part of her spine and brainstem dangled and dripped more blood onto the already saturated floor.

The thing held her head out like it was presenting it to me, and my instincts for self-preservation kicked in, taking complete control of my motor functions. I was already back in the house locking the front door before I even realized I had moved from the porch. I rushed to the living room and drug the armchair over to barricade the door with. The house was still thick with darkness, and nothing felt like it was real. Maybe it wasn't. Maybe I'd fallen asleep at the computer, and was having the most horrific lucid dream imaginable. I looked over at the computer desk, half expecting to see myself sitting in the chair, head back and snoring. The chair was empty, and I knew this wasn't a dream.

I grabbed a nearby end table and drug it over to the front door as well, keeping my head down so as not to accidentally glimpse the horror show on the porch through the window. I stopped dragging the table and listened to the suffocating silence. If the child creature wanted to get in, it wasn't trying to beat the front door down.

That's when I turned and ran to the kitchen.

I couldn't remember if I'd closed the back door when I burst through it earlier. I want to say I did, or at least I should have since I've never been one to leave doors open behind me. I had been in full-blown panic mode though, which meant I could have easily rushed in without-

I stopped short in the entrance of the kitchen. The back door was wide open, and cast a nearly imperceptible gray light across the floor from the ingress. It was enough for me to see small, muddy footprints tracked across the otherwise spotless linoleum.

Except it wasn't mud that had been tracked in, it was blood. And, the kitchen floor wasn't spotless; it was smattered in crimson drops of all sizes. I was still clutching the bat in my right hand, and brought my left hand up to the handle now, tightening my grip.

I wished I'd had the wherewithal to grab the good flashlight when I was out on the porch, but I don't even remember seeing it. Betsy had it turned off when I bolted through the door, catching her and the now late sheriff in some secret rendezvous disguised as a kind check-in for our wellbeing. Like he was doing me some *big favor*.

My mind flashed back to his body lying on the porch halfway disemboweled, and I saw the heavy duty police flashlight stuck firmly in his belt with all the other accessories that were useless to him now. I wasn't about to go back out through the front door just yet, but I made a mental note to grab the flashlight if I found myself back on the front porch. If I lived long enough to see the front porch again, that was.

I heard scratching behind me, and I whirled around with the bat, ready to swing first and ask questions later. I saw nothing behind me in the darkness, but still heard the scratching. It was coming from the far corner where Betsy had been working on the cat-house earlier.

My pupils strained to dilate further so I could see what horrid creature was lying in wait to pounce on me like it had the sheriff and Betsy. I took one slow and cautious step forward, and the source of the scratching came into focus.

It was Sandman scratching on one of the many carpeted areas of the palace Betsy was building for him. The cat gazed up at me with eyes of indifference, unaware of how close he came to getting his skull bashed in. I lowered the bat and Sandman uttered an apathetic meow before scaling the side of the half-built thing to disappear into a hole of one of the many cozy compartments. The back door slammed shut behind me, tearing a ragged gash through the heavy silence of the house, and I spun back around, readying the bat to strike again.

The echo of the door slamming decayed in seconds, leaving a single moment of silence right before I would never hear silence again. At first, all I could see were miniature shadows cast across the wall, but I felt their chilling presence closing in on me. I heard a cackle, followed by a clicking, tittering sound from all around me, and I couldn't tell if they were communicating or trying to disorient me.

Something swiped at my back, and yanked out my shirttail. I whirled around and swung the bat blindly, trying to put as much force behind it as I could. The bat connected only with air and my forward momentum sent me stumbling, but I was able to use the bat as a cane to steady myself before I fell.

Whatever swatted my back was only a distraction, because just as I put the end of the bat against the floor, something latched onto my leg. Before I could lift the bat to strike, it sunk its teeth into my calf, passing easily through the relaxed-fit denim to pierce the soft, pale flesh beneath.

I howled and brought the bat down hard without looking, gauging my aim by my pain. The meat of the bat connected, pinning the creature between it and the side of my calf, which only helped drive the cluster of fangs deeper into my leg. I gritted my teeth against the pain, brought the bat over my head, and this time looked down at the fucker. It was similar to the one from the porch, but smaller and more wiry. Its pale skin stood out against the darkness of the room, and I could tell it was wearing shreds of what years ago had been a Mickey Mouse t-shirt.

I swung hard at the thing, this time from the side, and the force of the blow unlatched the demon child's teeth, taking meaty, wet chunks of my leg with them. The thing rolled across the room, but recovered quickly, leaping to its feet and keeping its eyes locked on me. Its face was slick with my blood, which ran down its chin forming a puddle at its feet.

Another one of the creatures stepped out the darkness next to the one I'd just walloped from my leg, and then another one, and then another. Within seconds I was looking at six of the ghoulish children, each white as snow, and wearing remnants of what used to be clothing. They stared me down with different expressions that all communicated the same murderous intent.

I backed up a few steps, then turned and sprinted to the front door, where I pushed the couch out of the way with one hand while undoing the locks with the other, the bat tucked beneath my arm.

I didn't turn to look at the children because I could feel how close they were getting to me. When the final lock clicked from the frame, I tore the door open, leapt out, and slid in the blood that covered the entire porch. I struggled to get up and keep hold of the bat, but dropped it as I threw my hands out to keep from landing on my face. More blood splashed up as it hit the ground, bounced end over end behind me, and rolled to a stop next to the headless body of Betsy.

I landed hard on my knees but ignored the pain as I lunged back to grab the knob and pull the door shut. One of the creatures leapt toward the narrow opening a second too late and hit the backside of the door hard enough to rattle it on the hinges. Still on my knees, I crab-walked backwards away from the front door, expecting it to be flung back open with the children leaping out like clowns exiting a Volkswagen to finish me off. There was another hard smack from the other side of the door, which was either from another one of the things launching an ill-timed attack, or the one that nearly got through pounding with defiant frustration.

I pushed myself up, but slid again in the lake of blood my porch had become and landed hard on my chest. I didn't get the wind knocked out of me again, which I was grateful for since I didn't have time to recover from that again.

For a moment, I lay there on my chest, staring up at the front door waiting for it to explode from the frame, granting my would-be death dealers unobstructed access, but nothing happened. The door wasn't even that heavy or sturdy, and I was sure the things could rip right through it like wet tissue paper, but at the moment they weren't trying to. Besides, they were on the inside and could simply turn the knob to open the door if they wanted.

I didn't waste any more time waiting to see if the children had the wherewithal to understand how simple it was to get to me, and pushed myself to my feet, bracing against the wall to keep my balance. My hand came away leaving a bloody print against the heavily spattered wall like it was my contribution to a group art project. Since there was no further activity from the other side of the door, I figured they must have gone back out through the kitchen door, and were on their way around the house to head me off at the pass.

I scanned the ground around me for the bat, and found it up against the shoulder of my dead wife, close to where her head would have been if it wasn't sitting beside her currently. The bat was stained red from rolling through pints and pints of the intermingling blood of Betsy and the sheriff. I doubted that was the only bodily fluid that had been co-mingling between the two of them. I took two long but ginger strides to the bat, and picked it up without looking down at the headless Betsy.

We weren't the most perfect couple, and we'd had our share of the difficulties and differences that come with a long relationship, but despite her faults and apparent infidelities, she was my wife and I loved her. I didn't want my last image of her to be a headless corpse excreting essential life fluids on my shoes.

I used my shirt to wipe the blood from the handle of the bat, and it left a sticky, red film on the smooth, slick wood. It actually worked much like the pine-tar baseball players put on bats to improve their grip. I clutched it with both hands, flexing my fingers, and adjusting my grip to maximize the force of my swing. I'd only played two seasons of Little League in my youth, but I understood the concept of choking up on the handle to bring the meat of the bat around faster.

61

I'd been too focused on shutting the door, keeping my balance, and retrieving my weapon to notice grunts, clicks, and titters sounding all around me until it was too late. I imagine they'd been watching me from the darkness of the front yard, laughing amongst themselves at my comedy of errors as I struggled to maintain balance and control while convincing myself I was safe for the moment. The children were the ones in control now. Anything I did from here on out was of no consequence to them.

15

I felt the approach before contact was made. It wasn't a physically perceptible feeling, but more like a precognition of what was coming seconds before it did. The thing must have leapt at least twelve feet from the yard, over the porch banister, and onto my back. Its small, cold limbs wrapped around my torso, and clamped down with the released tension of a sprung bear trap.

The makeshift pine tar did me no good and the bat clattered to the ground again as my arms were pinned to my side by my pintsized attacker. I flashed back to what happened to the sheriff when one of these things got ahold of him in a similar fashion and I immediately began to flail about for lack of a better solution to my plight.

I might as well have stood stock-still for all the good struggling did for me. The fiendish child's legs clenched even harder around my midsection, forcing the air from my lungs, steadily increasing the pressure until my ribs screamed. They wouldn't be able to withstand much more without collapsing to make rib-kabobs of my vital organs. I felt tiny cold fingers begin to work their way around my neck, and panic shot through me, knowing I was seconds from joining the bloody pile of bodies on my porch.

Through the panic and awareness that my life was on the verge of coming to an end, I had a sudden moment of clarity, and came up with a seemingly obvious last ditch effort. The creature dug its nails into either side of my windpipe, and they punctured the flesh easily, like the thing had miniature surgical scalpels for fingers. I felt my neck become slick with my own blood I spun around, leapt a pathetic two inches into the air, and fell backwards, praying I hit the ground before my neck was peeled open like a fruit.

The child-beast absorbed the entirety of the impact as I brought the bulk of my measly hundred and sixty pounds down on top of it. We hit the concrete floor of the porch, splashing in blood like two kids wrestling in a thunderstorm. Several sharp pops like fireworks sounded in quick succession, ricocheted off the front of the house, and shot over the banister into the front yard. The razor-tipped, vise-like fingers released their grip from my neck, and the crushing power of the legs wrapped around me went slack, falling to my sides.

I wasted no time rolling off of my attacker, and scrambled to get to my feet, trying not to slip in blood again. My eyes darted around the porch looking first for the bat, which had rolled several feet over to the disemboweled sheriff, and then to the creature whose attack I had just successfully thwarted.

The thing wore a shredded sundress covered in flowers long faded to a dull gray. The skin, eyes, and snarl were the same as the others I'd seen, but its thin, stringy remnants of hair were pulled up on the sides of its head in two tragic looking pigtails.

The monster's chest had become a concave indention, and its neck was turned to the side at an unnatural angle. The child's black eyes were fixed in my direction but didn't see me anymore, and its tooth-filled maw was slightly agape. A string of reddish-brown drool dripped like taffy from a puller and mixed with the blood beneath its head. A slow hiss leaked from the partially spread, cracked, red lips of the creature, and I exhaled a breath I didn't realize I'd been holding right along with it.

From the darkness of the front yard came the clicks and growls of the other children, but louder and more furious than before, mixed with unsettling snarls that turned my stomach. I brought my hand to my neck to inspect the damage, and while it came back bloody, the wounds weren't deep enough to worry about at the moment.

The cacophonous frenzy in the yard grew louder, and I quickly but gingerly stepped over the lifeless beast to get the weapon I couldn't seem to keep a hold on. I took a step toward the bat, trying not to slip in blood or look at the pile of spindly gut-snakes piled atop the sheriff's chest and open stomach.

I went to lift my back leg, but it was stuck in place, rooted to the porch floor as five razor-sharp hornet stingers hooked their barbs into my ankle. I looked down before the pain had a chance to register, and saw tiny white fingers holding me tight in their snare. The thing flopped its head over to look at me, hanging limply to one side in a way that served to amplify my terror. I cried out and attempted to yank my leg from the child's piercing grasp, but it held fast while the claws dug in deeper.

I could feel my shoe filling with blood, and nearly passed out when I saw the spiked tips dig into my flesh up to the first knuckle. The indention in the child-creature's chest began to slowly push back out, sounding sharp snaps and cracks. Jagged, broken ribs tore easily through rotted flesh, leaving very little of it intact. The hobbled ghoul rolled on its side, and thick, black mucus crept slowly its nose to the floor like syrup trying to tease a pancake. A fetid muck of putrid, melted organs gently touched the floor, and began to mix with the blood.

The thing used its free arm to push itself slowly to its feet. If it weren't for the amount of adrenaline rushing through my system I would have already passed out from pain, or blood loss, or both. It was also the adrenaline that made me swing my unfettered leg around like a half-assed karate move, and knocked the legs back out from under the limp-necked fiend. This move also caused me to fall backwards, but my fall was broken by the bloated open cavity of the sheriff, now void of a small intestine.

I landed with a hard, wet smack against the hollowed-out man. It sounded like someone fist-fucking a six-foot pile of pudding. Then, for a moment, and only a moment, the child's grip loosened on my ankle as I brought my hand down on the sticky handle of the bat.

I lifted it with one hand, and brought it down hard on the thing's wrist, surprising myself with the precision and accuracy of the strike. The creature shrieked and released my ankle.

65

Suddenly free, I fell backwards over the sheriff's corpse, and rolled off onto my stomach, somehow managing to hold on to the bat this time.

A chorus of furious growls erupted from the lawn. I struggled to get to my feet, anticipating a full-blown attack. I pushed myself up on my arms but was unable to find purchase with my feet, and they slid outwards, contorting my legs into an awkward split. A pain shot through my groin like I was stabbed with a blade composed of electricity and fire. I'd pulled my groin once at football practice as a teenager, and remembered it being the worst pain I had experienced in life up to that point; it nagged on for weeks after the fact. If I made it out of this alive, I would revel in the pain, enjoying every excruciating moment, knowing the alternative was infinitely worse.

I blocked out the pain, steadied myself, and rose to my feet, fighting the slickness of blood mixed with the sheriff's viscera. My injured attacker rolled onto its chest, snapping the pointed ends off several protruding ribs in the process. The child was able to stand far easier than I, unaffected by the blood and bodily fluids beneath its feet. We faced each other now, separated by only four feet, both trying to anticipate the other's first move. The snarling growls grew closer while becoming steadily more frantic.

The creature's already tattered dress was coated in the thick, black stew of its rotted out insides, and its neck still hung gracelessly off to one side. The next few moments happened faster than my fear and adrenaline addled system could process, and I experienced it in quick flashes of action like flipping through a stack of photographs. The creature leapt to close the distance between us at the same moment I blindly swung the bat.

The meat of the bat connected with the thing's flopping head, surprising both of us. I opened my eyes to see the ghoul's limp body hit the bloody ground as its now detached head flew over the banister into the yard. The cacophonous calamity of the child's sisters and brothers reached a fevered pitch. I jumped the banister, and ran as fast as I could around the corner of the house

66

to the backyard. At least that's what I assumed had happened when I found myself leaning on the wall next to the back door, struggling to pull large gulps of air into my burning lungs.

16

I knew I wasn't safe.

All I'd done was extend my life by a minute or so while the children regrouped so they could converge on me while using the darkness to their advantage. I looked up and saw thick, green fog roll slowly up from the mouth of the open sinkhole. The pale yellow light still flashed lazily from the depths, but was muted by the fog.

The entire backyard smelled like stale death, and the fog left a film on my body that attached its stench to my skin. The shock and adrenaline had caused a high-pitch ringing in my ears I only just now became aware of, and I jammed a finger in my left ear desperately trying to dig it out. I took my finger out just in time for my ears to fill with a sound far worse than any ringing.

I heard heavy, wet breathing to my left, like someone was trying to unsuccessfully draw breaths through saturated earth. I turned to see one of the children who'd come through the open gate. It paused to size me up. Either that, or it wanted me to be aware of its presence before it attacked.

Thick drool dripped slowly from the half-open maw of the creature, explaining the wet sound accompanying each shallow breath. I recognized the shredded Mickey Mouse t-shirt of the child I'd fled the house earlier to get away from, and saw in its exaggeratedly round, black eyes the thing didn't intend on letting me get away again. The creature clenched its slender white fingers into snowball-like fists and leapt at me.

I had no time to bring the bat back to swing with any force, and instead reached for the knob on the back door, turned it, and fell in on the hard, cold linoleum of the kitchen. As I was falling I caught a glimpse of the creature flying past the now open door, turning its head mid-air to see how I had eluded it. I pulled my feet the rest of the way inside, and kicked the door shut. The creature screamed in frustration as it beat against the door, trying to knock it off its hinges as I sprang up and turned the lock.

I started limping across the kitchen, taking only three steps before the banging stopped. I paused and for the first time was able to feel the tremendous pain in my ankle. I looked down to see the trail of blood I was leaving across the white linoleum floor like a painter's first brush stroke on a clean, new canvas. The adrenaline was either wearing off, or the pain had become too intense to be overridden by the rush of the naturally occurring chemicals in my brain.

The throbbing inferno of pain from the wounds in my ankle climbed all the way to my brain, took center stage, and demanded to be addressed. The bleeding had slowed since my initial wounding, but was still flowing freely at a lazy pace. If I didn't at least attempt to stop the bleeding, I'd pass out from blood loss soon enough, and become easy pickings for the children from the hole. A light tapping against the window over the sink inadvertently drew my gaze up to my personal porthole into hell.

What I saw caught me so off guard, I was already falling backward before I realized I'd tripped over my own feet. I reached out to grab the back of one of the kitchen table's chairs to catch my balance, but succeeded only in pulling the chair down on top of me. I pushed the chair from my chest, and propped myself up on my elbows, desperate to confirm what I thought I saw.

The thing staring in at me from the window looked similar to the monster children, but was not one of them. What flesh remained on its face was in sporadically placed patches, stretched thin to the point of translucency. There was more skull showing through than skin left to cover it all, like a picture you'd find in a school's biology textbook, but there was nothing to be learned from this gruesome image.

69

I initially thought the thing was staring down at me through the misty glass, but I wasn't sure, seeing as this creature lacked the sinister black orbs for eyes the children possessed. There were in fact no eyes, or anything else occupying the dark holes of the skull-faced creature meant for ocular housing. There was a short-brimmed hat sitting askew atop the rotted head of the thing, with wispy of strands of thin, white hair peeking out from beneath. There were no lips to speak of around its mouth, leaving clenched and crooked yellow teeth exposed in a frightfully ironic grin.

This thing was like the children but not completely, and the cap it was wearing sparked a sudden realization in my fear and pain-addled mind. It was the kind of hat that went with a uniform worn by bus drivers years before schools started letting fat, lazy, pill-addicted hillbillies haul around the town's most precious cargo. I was staring right into the hollow eyeholes of the poor soul who had been driving the bus.

The driver's teeth separated and its bottom jaw fell open as if it was attempting to speak, but all that came from the rotted mouth was a puff of the same green fog rising from the hole, followed by a millipede far bigger than I ever thought they could get in Texas. It was thick like a summer sausage, and used its many legs to creep up to the left of the driver's face for only a moment before forcing itself through the hole that had once been covered by a nose.

The sight was enough to trigger another adrenaline dump, allowing me to stand without succumbing to the ever-increasing pain in my ankle. I clutched the handle of the bat hard enough to make my knuckles crack and bleed, but I knew the weapon wasn't going to be enough to do any significant damage to the beasts I was up against. I was going to need to find a more efficient implement of death if I was going to stand a chance against my undead enemies.

The bus driver brought his head back a few inches before slamming it forward into the window. The blow wasn't hard enough to break all the way through, but hairline cracks were already beginning to work their way out from the point of impact, racing against each other to get to the edge first. Another crash sounded from the other side of the house, announcing the creatures coming back through the front door to head me off at the pass.

I cut back through my own trail of blood, leaking more than enough along the way to cover any footsteps I was leaving. Directly across from the back door was the door to the basement. There aren't many basements in Texas, particularly in East Texas on account of how close it is to the coastline. We lucked out since the couple who owned our house years ago, the original owners, were a tad paranoid about certain missiles being pointed at us by certain countries. They took the steps necessary to properly build out and reinforce a basement. The realtor told me the couple had planned to turn it into a full on bomb shelter after saving up enough money for materials. The threat of being nuked ended before that could happen, so it remained a regular old basement.

We used it as a laundry room and general storage space, primarily occupied by half-finished, cat-related projects Betsy had either given up on or pledged to continue at a later date. I also kept a few yard-work related tools stowed away in the small space allotted to me. I would find what I needed there.

There was no lock on the basement door, and I flew down the steps as quickly as I could without making any noise against the old wood planks. I hoped the children would think I went through the back door, and continue their pursuit, thusly buying me some time, but I couldn't count on it. For all I knew the basement was already crawling with those things, and I was plunging headlong into certain death.

I hit the basement floor flatfooted and stifled a groan as I groped at the darkness above me for the string attached to a single bare bulb, which was the sole source of light in the basement. Betsy had me run the power for the basement to a separate breaker so the main wouldn't trip when she used the washer and dryer at the same time, and I hoped those bastards

71

hadn't compromised it as well. I found it and pulled flinching at the sudden burst of light above me. Success! I scanned the small space, looking for children hiding amongst the mess, but the coast was clear as far as I could tell. I grabbed a t-shirt from the basket of clean clothes on top of the dryer, and tore it into strips as I quickly maneuvered through the creations of Betsy that would forever remain unfinished.

On the floor in the far corner, I found the large, wooden toolbox my father had given me as a wedding present years ago. Inside it was a spool of twine for the weed-eater, the screwdriver I use to change sparkplugs in the lawnmower, and a machete I'd bought to hack off the ivy that had taken over a portion of the fence. I never got to use it, though, because a cold snap hit before I had a chance, and killed off the ivy for me. I let the bat fall to the floor, replacing it in my hand with the smooth, cold handle of my new salvation.

17

I threw aside the heavy, canvas sheath in which the machete had been residing since its purchase. The price tag was still attached by way of a thin, plastic loop run through the woven material of the covering. I passed the blade back and forth between my hands, getting used the weight of it, and took a few practice swings for good measure. The machete was way lighter than the bat, and I was able to bring it around much faster. I was pleased with the decision to upgrade my weapon, but it wouldn't do me much good if I didn't make it out of the basement alive to use it.

The machete felt so good in my hands it was hard to put it back down, but I set it close beside me as I crouched to take a knee. I took one of the longer pieces from the torn t-shirt, wrapped it around my bleeding ankle, and tied the tightest knot I could, pulling the fabric until the pain was accompanied by the dull throb of reduced circulation. It wasn't the best fix, but it would do until I could seek proper medical attention. Or, rather, if I had the chance to seek proper medical attention.

A bang followed by a commotion of clatter came from overhead, letting me know the children were in the kitchen again. My plan to fool them into thinking I went out the back door must have worked, or otherwise they would've been down in the basement long before I had a chance to get the machete. It sounded like they were tearing apart the kitchen, thinking I must be hidden somewhere amongst the table and chairs, or crouched in a cabinet below the sink. It would only be a matter of seconds before the lilywhite abominations noticed the basement door and put two and two together.

I tiptoed quickly through the piles of junk like a ballerina who missed her cue, and stood in front of the old wooden stairs.

I reached out for the string and pulled to extinguish the light. The door at the top of the steps flung and the basement was flooded with the growls, clicks, and grunts of the children. They were growing impatient with our game of hide-and-seek.

I ducked to the side of the stairs and crouched in the darkness, ready to spring, my machete cocked back like a cobra waiting for the perfect moment to strike. The creatures wasted no time bounding blindly down the stairs, confident in their assumption of where I was hiding. I didn't dare peek around the steps for fear of giving up my position, and with it the element of surprise.

It was dark as death in the basement, but as far as I knew the children had been trapped in darkness for years. I assumed they had adapted by now, and were able to see in the dark as well as I could see in the light. I could have been wrong, but I wasn't ready to risk my life to test the hypothesis. I would have to trust my ears to help calculate their proximity based on their rushed, heavy steps and furious, wet panting.

A moment later, I leapt around to the base of the steps, swinging the machete while pulling the string to again ignite the single bulb at the base of the stairs. My hope was the sudden burst of light would serve to disorient the children, and give me more time to hack away at them.

The blade sang a sweet, sharp whine as it sliced through the air on its maiden voyage. I hadn't accounted for the time it would take for my eyes to adjust to the light, but they did just in time to see the machete strike the banister. The vibration from hitting something so solid stung my hand, and advanced up my arm, and into my shoulder. The machete bounced off the banister, flew from my grasp, and skidded across the basement floor, coming to a stop against the wall next to were I had just been hiding.

Something landed on the floor in front of me and slid up against my shins. I jumped, slamming the small of my back against the dryer behind me, expecting to be mauled at any moment. I bit down against the pain in my spine, and

74

inadvertently chewed halfway through the tip of my tongue as I looked down to see what had landed in front of me. At my feet was the headless body of the creature I had encountered on the front porch, its limbs bent and twisted into impossible angles. The thick, black insides spilled out and pooled around the broken thing.

I heard the clicks and snarls of the children, only now the tone and cadence mimicked laughter. I looked up to see the monster in the Mickey Mouse t-shirt standing at the top of the steps with four more of the pale, evil children behind him. I suddenly realized they'd thrown the broken, headless body of one of their own down the stairs as a ploy to drive me out of hiding. I blinked, and in that instance the four children behind Mickey Mouse shirt had leapt from the top step, and were flying through the air right at me. Mickey Mouse remained at the top, having sent in the lackeys to do his dirty work.

I dove to my left, surprised by my own reflex and agility, just before the flying children were about to collide with me. In quick succession, they one at a time smacked against the dryer, landing atop the body of their decapitated comrade in a pile of gnashing teeth and spindly, white fingers grasping at empty air.

I didn't escape unscathed though. The first of the flying children had reached out and swiped at my arm, and I could already feel the burning of a fresh wound before I hit the floor and slid up against the wall. I glanced down to see blood running down my arm from four evenly spaced gashes just above my bicep. I wasn't sure how much more damage I could take before the adrenaline wouldn't be enough to keep me conscious and moving.

Beneath my freshly wounded arm was the machete I thought I had lost for good, being covered now in my freely flowing blood. There was no more time to think about anything. I needed to act or die. I grabbed the machete by the handle and jumped up from the floor in one fluid movement. While the children, tangled up amongst each other, were growling and fighting to stand up, I ducked under the banister, and dashed up the steps, brandishing the bloody machete.

I expected Mickey Mouse to launch himself at me, which was why I held the machete out hoping to impale him midair. I was actually relieved to see he was no longer lurking in the doorway at the top of the stairs, but the feeling was short lived. He knew he had me trapped down in the basement, and even after narrowly averting the attack of his henchmen, he could have come down behind them and finished me off easily. Not only did he not come after me, he'd disappeared completely, which meant he wanted me to follow him. Despite knowing I was quite possibly running headlong to my ultimate demise, I had no choice.

The first footfalls of the now detangled children smacked hard against the first step, and were mere feet behind me a second later. I took the last steps two at a time, and crashed into the darkness of the kitchen, swiping the air in front of me with the machete. I slowed up enough to bang my hip into the counter at only half the speed I was initially traveling, and winced but wasted no time taking further stock of my growing list of injuries.

I had no time to close the door to at least slow the group's pursuit, so I continued through the kitchen, jabbing randomly into the darkness hoping to get lucky. I unsuccessfully tried to ignore the now shattered kitchen window, but noticed the bus driver was no longer on the other side of it.

I made it through the kitchen with four monsters hot on my heels, and as I ran through the next room, I saw Sandman's eyes peering out from the safety of another cat-house that would never be finished. I cursed the cat as I sprinted past, feeling the pain from my ankle begin to protest against the strain of running. Down the hall in front of me was the front door, wide open, unobstructed, and as far as I could see free of Mickey.

Seeing the open door gave me hope although I didn't know why. Even when I passed over the threshold, the four beasts would be only paces behind me, and I was probably running into an ambush and certain death. I had no other choice though, and if I made it through the door I at least had a chance, albeit slim, of actually getting away.

I was about a foot or so from the open door when I decided to cover those last feet and more by leaving my feet. I leapt like I was going for the long distance jump record in high school, which was the last time I'd participated in any kind of organized sport. My momentum carried me much farther than I expected to fly, and in that half of a moment I felt like a superhero.

I had no plan for when my feet touched the ground, but I'd found during this time of extreme stress my brain was able to think faster using all of its power to focus on one thing only: survival. My mind used every bit of the limited, public education I'd received to calculate my options within nanoseconds of landing. If I stuck the landing without my momentum sending me head over heels, and continued traveling forward at my current rate of speed or faster, I would only need to take two steps before jumping the four steps leading down from the porch.

If I was able to pull off that feat of athleticism, my plan was to run through the lawn and out to the street, where I would continue running north, hoping to see a car I could flag down, or make it to the all night convenience store two blocks down. If I made it there and the children were still following, I would at least have the benefit of light to help me combat them. This all depended on my being able to pull it off without falling, or being brought down from behind by a band of monster children.

As I soared across the ingress and began my descent, I saw something out of the corner of my eye that drew my focus. Standing at the right of the door was Mickey Mouse t-shirt, lying in wait just as I'd suspected. He narrowed his eyes, turning the large, black spheres into thin, angry slits. I looked forward again a single moment before my foot touched down on the porch.

I wished I had thought not to land on the foot attached to my mangled ankle.

77

18

When my foot touched down on the blood-covered porch, my injured ankle refused to accept and support the weight behind it. My ankle bent at an angle it was never meant to, and I'm sure I would have heard the bone snap if my ears weren't ringing from the sudden excruciating pain. Adrenaline could no longer push the pain away, and the best I could hope for now was to go into shock and die before hitting the ground.

My knee gave out and my leg bent up behind me like a soggy French fry. I fell backwards, landing on it. As painful as it was, it kept the back of my head from smacking against the floor hard enough to scramble my brains, and punch my ticket. I wish it could've been that easy.

The blood-slicked floor aided my forward momentum and I slid on my back to the steps, then tumbled down them. On a positive note, my plan had halfway worked, but this was an all or nothing situation unfortunately. I had made it down the steps and into the front yard, but due to my significant impairment, I wouldn't be able to get any farther.

I flinched, waiting for the children to descend on me any second and tear me apart one chunk at a time. I coughed a fine, red mist into the stale, still air above my face, letting me know I'd broken at least one rib, and pierced a lung. Hot needles of pain bore through my chest from the inside out as I coughed again, sending another crimson cloud up into the darkness.

I closed my eyes and held my breath, hoping the first blow from whichever child got to me first was the one that killed me. After a few seconds when nothing had happened, I opened my eyes, and released my breath, wheezing through a lung full of blood. My body was being held together by pain so intense my brain couldn't process it correctly, and distorted the powerful sensation. I wouldn't say I was comfortable, but at least I felt . . . used to it.

Turning my head was out of the question, so I rolled my eyes back toward the porch steps to see what was delaying my demise. The four children who'd pursued me through the house stood perched on the porch just above the first step, hissing and snarling. I followed the light reflecting off their billiard-ball-eyes, and turned my gaze around to see what had caught their attention.

Standing next to the leg not currently crumpled up beneath me was Mickey Mouse t-shirt. Gripped tightly in a hand too small to wrap all the way around the handle was my machete. His mouth was pulled back tight against his face in a smile that rocked the juices in my belly.

He cast a look up at the children on the porch, letting them know to stay where they were, then he scowled at the machete and tossed it over his shoulder. It landed softly somewhere behind him in the long, cool grass.

He walked up to my head and I tried to call out, but all I could manage was a blood-addled coughing fit. My mouth tasted like alkaline-laced spoiled meat, and tips of dead batteries. Mickey, the child who seemed to wield some sort of dominion over his cohorts, stood directly over me, and glared down with the face of a rotted, sun-bleached jack-o-lantern. I could only wiggle my fingers as a form of protest and self-defense, a useless tactic when dealing with a monster.

I wanted to tell the child to just kill me already, but all I could muster was another gurgling cough as I continued to slowly drown ironically in a substance known for giving life. With how much I had already bled this evening, I was honestly surprised I had enough left in me to fill an entire lung. Spots began to form across my vision, blotting out the child's awful, staring face. In the distance, I could hear a slurping sound I realized was me trying to breathe.

My eyelids fluttered, serving to blink away the spots long enough for me to see the other four children had left the

79

porch to join their leader, and were now staring down at me with death mask faces. Mickey bent down and put his face inches from mine, and the smell of death and sadness poured from the child like a wretchedly polluted stream.

A cantankerous moan sounded off to the side of me, and all six of us turned our eyes toward it. Stumbling around the side of the house was the skeletal bus driver. I could see the bottom half of his shirt had been long since ripped to shreds, with only a few tattered scraps left dangling over an open and empty stomach cavity. I briefly envisioned the trapped children ripping out the helpless driver's insides to feed on ages ago.

A brief glimmer of hope blossomed in my dying mind that the stomach-less driver represented my salvation, and held the only key in controlling the tiny beasts. Perhaps there was some mystic clock that was about to expire, giving them no choice but to return to the bus, which would allow me to either painfully crawl to the phone, or die in peace. As the driver staggered closer, it became obvious he was not my savior, but was instead coming to join the children in my demise.

I don't know if I closed my eyes, but either way I could no longer see as I felt intense pressure close in around my neck. Five icy darts dug their way into the wounds inflicted earlier on the same area, but this time there was no escape. The pressure grew, filling my head with the sound of a rushing freight train getting louder by the second ... until it just stopped.

I couldn't truly feel the hands and mouths of the children and the driver as they tore into my chest and stomach. It was more like a phantom sensation that didn't cause pain, but released it from my body instead. I was flooded with a sense of relief as I felt myself wrapped in a fog of warmth come to carry me away. The troubles of life were over, and I never realized how much I worried about things until my cares drifted away all at once.

Time was non-existent for me now, and the only thing I was able to feel was the warmth of finality wrapping me up in a cocoon of protection. Then, all at once the warmth was gone, replaced by a chilling cold from not only around me, but inside as well. The sensation grew impossibly frigid until it burned away the remaining consciousness left connecting me to the world I was accustomed to. Then, I felt nothing at all.

EPILOGUE

The next morning, workers from the city showed up in two trucks loaded with equipment to aid in their daily duties of filling potholes, clearing road debris, and whatever they thought would help them deal with a sinkhole. Having never fixed a sinkhole before, they brought extra shovels, rakes, and two wheelbarrows, all of which they would find to be useless. Not only because dealing with the hole would require far more to remedy than a few garden tools, but also because of the scene they walked into.

Reggie's body lay at the bottom of the porch steps, mutilated beyond recognition. His body was completely pulled apart from his neck to his groin, and while blood was everywhere, his organs were absent. The first worker who walked up and saw the sickening sight of the hollowed out homeowner nearly fainted before turning around to projectile vomit the eggs, bacon, and waffles he and the crew had just eaten at the diner in town.

He gasped between heaves, trying to tell the others to call the sheriff, but it took another worker running up and peering over his shoulder to get the message. He turned away before tossing his breakfast as well, pulled out his cellphone, and called the sheriff. He heard ringing close by, which stopped at the same time the call went to voicemail. The worker hung up, looked around the yard, and then called again. The ringing started up again, and was coming from the porch, so he let the phone keep ringing as he followed the sound.

Three other workers were running up to see what was going on, and two of them joined their fellow up-chucker in heaving still warm meals onto the grass at their feet. The man with the phone walked around the body of Reggie, making sure to not look down, and followed the ringing up the steps. When he reached the top and took in the scene, he dropped the phone, and joined the choir of puking happening on the lawn.

When the workers were able to collect themselves, a call was made to the police department, and within minutes the home was swarming with officers. They locked the scene down, not letting anyone who wasn't an officer or medic past the perimeter they'd created with bright yellow police tape where the lawn met the street. Members of the local media and an ever-growing crowd of lookey-loos gathered in front of the home trying to get a glimpse of what all the fuss was about.

The police had covered Reggie's mangled body with a sheet so as not to expose the man's grisly demise, and you couldn't see over the banister of the porch from the street, leaving the curious crowd in the dark as to what had happened. When an officer would enter or leave the perimeter, a bevy of questions would be hurled their way, to which 'no comment' would be said over and over until out of earshot.

Investigators filled the house, poring over the entirety of the scene trying to make some sort of sense out of it all. There were no signs of anyone besides the three deceased anywhere in the entire house, save for a cat wandering between rooms, apathetic to the bustling activity. When they checked the backyard to inspect the sinkhole, which was the reason the city workers were dispatched to the home in the first place, they found an opening in the ground half filled with dirt and chunks of hard, red clay.

When the children returned to the bus that had become their eternal prison, the walls of the sinkhole collapsed, covering their existence once again. Eventually, the authorities had to let the public know what was going on, and they did in a statement that evening made by Officer George Green, who was the acting sheriff for the moment.

With no evidence or explanation as to how three people came to be so incredibly mutilated, the authorities decided to spin the story so as not to cause a massive panic in the town. The

83

official statement delivered to the public was that a murder/suicide took place at the residence when Reggie discovered his wife was having an affair with the sheriff.

Officer Green stated they had surmised from their extensive investigation that Reggie apparently discovered his wife and the sheriff locked in a compromising position on the porch. He then confronted the two, during which a struggle broke out between the two men, leading to Reggie killing the sheriff, his wife, and then himself.

Green was immediately hit with an avalanche of questions, none of which he answered, instead stating that was all the information he could give at this time before leaving the podium. The media frenzy continued for a week after the incident occurred, but no further questions were answered, and no one was granted access to the scene until the bodies were removed and the house was thoroughly cleaned. Eventually, the hype died down and the scandal was forgotten with the development of other more important news happening in the world.

No one noticed the dump trunks filled with dirt going back and forth from the house as the city worked to fill the rest of the sinkhole. The house remained dark and empty until it was decided by the mayor to bulldoze the property in an attempt to erase any memory of the awful event.

When the house was gone, the property was reduced to a dirt-covered empty lot. It stayed that way for years until two young newlyweds bought the property from the city, and began to build their dream house. They wouldn't come to notice the uneven indention in the middle of their backyard until years later.

For more JOHN WAYNE COMUNALE and many other great
authors, check out **AND HELL FOLLOWED** and
BREAKING BIZARRO!

deathsheadpress.com

Made in the USA
Middletown, DE
10 March 2022